The Collective

By
Thomas A. Cerra

Copyright © 2024 NATIVE BOOK PUBLISHERS

All rights reserved. No part of this book may be used, reproduced, scanned, or distributed in any printed or electronic form by no means whatsoever without written permission. Please do not copyright materials in violation of the author's right. Purchase only authorized editions. For more information, e-mail all inquiries to info@Nativebookpublishers.com.Published by Native Book Publishers.

www.nativebookpublishers.com

Printed in United States of America

Table Of Contents

The Collective 1

Murder at Lily Lake 6

Little Man 36

Heartbroken 61

The Shallow Hours 86

"Brown House" 93

"Help Wanted" 133

"An Autumn Tale" 145

"Wyndam" 154

"Morpheus" 174

Dedication

I proudly and with all my heart

Dedicate this book

To my siblings.

To my sisters

Kathie Smith and Louise Cali

Who left us much too early.

To Joseph Thrasher

Aimee Teitsworth

And Dorothy Cerra,
my older siblings and

Truly my oldest friends.

To my brother's

Christopher and Anthony Cerra

Whom I played with as children

Partied with often

And who endured me

At my very worst.

I love you all!

Also, a special remembrance

To my little sister Marie

Who never got a chance to live!

You are not forgotten.

Acknowledgment

I would like to acknowledge my daughter Maura Cerra for the artwork she contributed including the cover art.

To see more of her art go to Illustrations by Mo

mauracerra@gmail.com

I'd also like to acknowledge Aimee Teitsworth for assisting with editing, my brother Anthony Cerra for being a creative springboard and Renee Zuraski for proofreading. Their contributions meant more than they know.

The Collective

The abysmal forest!

Illimitable, unbounded,

Immeasurable, Infinite,

But...Not impenetrable.

Entrance... Through its gray skin;

A haze scented with decay

And ageless as the clouds

Allows no path to follow,

No guide nor map.

Attainable... To any
foolishly fearless.

Yet respect it

No matter what the mindset

Or its darkness

Will absorb your essence

Resolved to be a faction

Of its substance.

Once in...

You will hear your heartbeat.

As the white noise

Diminishes with the light

And thus, your pulse

Last remains

To echo in your ears.

To say there is no light

Is a fallacy of sorts.

Fine thin strands

Like fishing line pulled tautly

Pierce the tangled canopy of limbs.

Where these fair flecks touch...

A flower is born;

A gift from the mother

To the sun.

Something else,

Birthed of black wood

Is that...

Formed of shadow and light

That...

A spirit spawned

Of the boscage and

Cloaked in the folds of the dim.

That...

Which moves with the morning fog

As the sun rises

And the stars are emptied

From the blush

Of indigo sky.

What drags these

But the weight of the day

In the dark regions

Where nimble flits

Of eyes remain disguised

In the thicket.

The spirit celebrates life

At its finest,

With flowers flowing

From its heart.

Lilies floating

Across the forest floor.

Moving only by the grace

Of a breeze so faint

And delicate

It belies the human touch.

Those that enter

Without malice

May leave undisturbed.

Those whose corrosive way

Shall stay to realize

What is best and what is least.

Thus, their substance

Imprisoned

As a toadstool on a damp log,

Moss on a northward tree

Or a fern sipping

The dew of the morning.

Protected through time

By the spirit.

Born of the mother,

Grained by the light,

Shades of the dim.

Eternal.

The End

Murder at Lily Lake

I'd been driving for a while, hours actually. I wasn't really going anywhere; just had to get away from where I was and who I was with. She was a torturing, castrating bitch, bossy and belligerent; the type of person that could find fault with the littlest thing and turn that into a daylong rant. Often, her divisive behavior began at sunrise and ended when she closed her eyes to sleep.

What made her this way? I don't know. She would blame me, the way she blamed me for everything from the cold in winter to the weeds in the garden. Nothing bad was beyond my evil powers. Those who knew her prior to me said she was always a difficult person and just got worse as she got older. They admired me for my overwhelming patience.

However, there is only so much one can take. There is nothing worse than swallowing the same shit day after day. Eventually, you need to put the fork down and say enough is enough.

This morning I'd eaten my last chunk of crap when I got berated for buttering the morning toast incorrectly. How the fuck does one butter toast incorrectly? This fifteen-minute tirade, I answered with a stiff middle finger and sarcastic sayonara as I strolled out the door, hopped in my car and sped off.

I don't think she saw it coming, and I certainly don't believe she knew that it was permanent. I heard her endless stream of carping in the background as I walked out, but for the life of me, I had no idea what she was saying. Her words melded into one high-pitched clamor beyond the ears' ability to decipher. This would be the last I would hear of her, and thank God for that.

Springsteen said it best, "I went out for a ride, and I never went back. "Like a river that don't know where it's flowin, I took a wrong turn and just kept goin" I kept goin' and never planned to see that house or that bitch ever again. Where I was flowin' to, I didn't know; just knew I wasn't ever going back to that misery.

I had money, enough to get me by for a while anyway. My work was my writing, and I could do that anywhere. What I didn't have was a story. Sitting in that house, being nagged to death, had built one large immovable block. Since no story was coming to me, maybe by hitting the road, I'd find one somewhere out there in that vast collection of scenarios people call life.

Life, what the hell is it? I remember it as a board game when I was a kid, but I hadn't lived in years. I think I stopped playing when I started accepting. It's like a trap you step into, but no matter how much you want to, you refuse to chew off your leg to save the rest of you. Everything begins to die, not from the leg up, but from the head down. Then, when you finally realize you're on the threshold of oblivion, you haven't the strength or courage to do what needs to be done.

I realized it, and I ran, fortunately, with both legs and balls intact. I picked a direction I'd never gone, taking a road I'd never been on, searching for someplace I'd never seen. All I wanted was to find something that would replace the images of the prison and the warden I'd left behind. Didn't know how long this might take, maybe days, months, or, God help me, years. I begged to see some type of huge mental eraser waiting just around the next bend.

The remains of a sudden rainstorm steamed off the asphalt just before sunset. The sun turned white and then disappeared into the thickening forest. Still, I found no eraser, although the road had bent a dozen times. Two hours into the evening, I began to feel hungry and in need of a restroom. I came around a long-sloping turn and found a bar/restaurant sitting in among a canopy of pines.

I brought the car to a roll and eased into the crowded parking lot. I'd been told that a crowded parking lot at a restaurant means good food. Who told me this, I could not recall, that odd faceless someone who knows all and shares their wealth of knowledge from afar. I hoped this omnipotent spirit spouted the truth. I longed for a nice meal and a cold lager to wash it down. Maybe a second lager with a good cigar would be nice, too, something to celebrate my newfound freedom. But that might be asking a bit too much of a place sitting on the edge of nowhere.

When I entered...the dining room was bustling. I only waited a few moments, however, before the host greeted me and showed me to a small booth in the far corner. The waitress came to me quickly with a menu and a pleasant smile. I asked for a lager and directions to the men's room. By the time I returned, my lager and a frosted mug were waiting for me. 'A nice treat,' I thought. 'Perfect for a hot summer night.'

Dinner was excellent: pot roast, fresh mashed potatoes with lots of gravy. Comfort food that reminded me of Mom's Sunday dinners when I was a kid. Afterward, as I paid my check, I asked for directions to the bar section. The server pointed to a door at the far end of the dining area. I thanked her and gave her a more than adequate tip, to which she smiled widely and thanked me. By her reaction, I assumed the tips in this place weren't often as generous as the server would have liked, so I dropped another five on her and thanked her again.

Behind the door was a long, narrow, dimly lit hallway with additional restrooms on the left. There was a noticeable aroma of urine and bleach coming from them, and the floor was sticky. 'Quite different from the pristine facilities on the other side of the dining area,' I thought. The tackiness diminished slightly as I entered the bar room, a smoke-laden, dank, brown expanse with a polished wood L-shaped bar and a high-beamed ceiling. While the dining room was bright, clean and inviting, this place made me feel dirty as soon as I entered.

I located a seat on the opposite side of the bar and ordered that second lager. The bartender plopped the bottle down in front of me and said, "Two bucks," then wiped his nose with the back of his hand. I thought, 'what? No frosted mug, no pleasant smile?' I could see this guy wasn't in the mood. Maybe it was just too hot, or maybe he had met my ex. That would make anyone miserable.

As I lifted my beer to take my first drink, I took notice of movement in the shadows just to the right of me at the very end of the bar. The flame of a lighter illuminated the face of a woman with a cigarette pinched between her lips. I tried hard not to stare, but the harder I tried, the more I did. It wasn't until she glimpsed up and saw my eyes upon her that I turned away.

"What you lookin' at?"

"Nothing. Please, pardon me, I didn't mean to."

"Oh, relax. You want to stare, stare. I got nothing to hide."

In that short but profound look I noticed much about this strange woman buried in the shadows. She may not have had anything to hide, but she was most certainly hiding, her eyes alight with loss and loneliness and her expression as distant as the moon.

"You're sizing me up, aren't you? You think with one look you know who I am, some lonely lush you can have for a few drinks and a charming line or two. Well, you might be right, but the lines better be damn convincing."

"No, I wasn't thinking that at all."

That's what I said, but she wasn't wrong. I wanted a change, and what better way to accomplish that than the pleasures of a perfect stranger?

She changed seats and moved in beside me, pulling her ashtray and her wine glass along with her. I sipped at my beer and watched her as she gathered up her things and slipped them into her purse. As she worked, I measured more of her: the color of her hair and the shape of her lips. I found myself drawn to the nape of her neck, wanting to taste it, nibble at it like a late-night snack. Again, she noticed my glare and smiled.

"Were you lookin' down my shirt?"

"No, of course not."

"It's OK. I'll show 'em to you if you'd like. I don't have much. They're more push-up bra and padding than anything."

She began unbuttoning her blouse. The bartender noticed and told her to stop.

"Buddy, if she's bothering you, I'll toss her."

"No, she's fine. We are just getting acquainted."

"Acquainted," she snarled, "Dusty here is gonna have to look that word up."

"Listen, Veri, any trouble from you and you're out of here tonight, you hear me?"

"It's OK, Dusty is it, and she isn't any trouble."

I slipped Dusty a five spot, and he headed to the other side of the bar, but not before he filled up this woman's wine glass from a bottle he had stashed under the bar.

"Don't pay any attention to him. He's been bartending here ever since I've been drinking here. How long has that been, Dusty?"

"Two days," he shouted back without looking.

"See, we've been pals for forty-eight hours and already know each other better than most, right Dusty?"

"Give it a rest, will you, Veri?"

"Veri, that's an odd name," I interrupted.

"Well, it's actually Veronica, but that's so long and old-sounding. I prefer being called Veri. It is short and sweet, like me."

She wasn't lying. Veri was barely taller than the barstool; I would guess she stood about five foot one. Although she spoke coarsely, her words sang with a childlike resonance, sweet yet sultry all at once. I realized I already liked her, and I didn't even know her. Maybe it was because she was erasing the image of old Bulla butt pucker, the warden whack job I'd left in my rearview this morning. Maybe it was something else, though, and I just hadn't figured it out.

She finished her glass of wine as I sucked down the last of beer number two. Veri flagged down Dusty for a refill and another round for me. It dawned on me right then that I hadn't had my cigar.

"Dusty, you wouldn't happen to sell cigars at this establishment?"

"Establishment?" Veri laughed.

"Where's that dictionary? Dusty's confused again."

Dusty was a well-built man with sandy brown hair and a three-day stubble. Everything about him told me he didn't much like his life either. If he had a sense of humor, he didn't bring it to work with him. Maybe he was overworked and underpaid, like the majority of the world, and his bitterness had just caught up with him.

"Shut the hell up, Veri. It's a bar, buddy and, yeah, we have cigars. What kind do you want?"

"I didn't mean to annoy you. What type have you got?"

"We have the good, the fair, and the rolled horseshit. Which would you like?"

"The good, absolutely!"

Dusty pulled from a shelf above the register a small wooden box and brought it over to me.

"Eight bucks apiece."

I picked up one and sniffed it. Not that I'd know a good cigar from a bad, but I figured if it had a nice fresh scent, it would be worth the eight dollars. This did. I handed Dusty a ten. "Keep the change."

He stuck the ten in his pocket, refilled Veri's glass, and then returned the box to its shelf. A minute later, he returned with a pair of cigar scissors and snipped the end for me. Dusty struck a stick match, and I puffed, tasting the smooth flavor and listening to the subtle crackle as the leaves caught.

There is something very satisfying and relaxing about a fine cigar. Truth was, I didn't know a fine cigar from a stale cigarette, but this felt good, and that was really all that mattered. But I'm being redundant. Although I'm pretty sure a stale cigarette would not have elicited the same pleasing response, this was, as I had hoped, a true feeling of freedom.

"You seem to be really enjoying that cigar. Am I not your type?"

"What is that supposed to mean?"

"Well, you're treatin' that thing like a lover, so I thought maybe that's what you like."

"Oh, Jesus Christ, Veri, you just ruined this cigar for me. No, I'm not like that. I am celebrating."

"Celebrating? With a cigar? What are you celebrating?"

"Freedom, the start of a new life, living after being comatose for years. Actually, all of the above."

"Sounds like you just broke up with someone."

"Yes, that is certainly what it sounds like, doesn't it?"

"Why a cigar and not say, a glass of champagne?"

"When a child is born, a man smokes a cigar."

I could see Veri thinking about this as she sipped her wine. She didn't say anything for a while as I sat back, rolling the cigar smoke in my mouth. She watched as I blew a large grey smoke ring that glided across the barroom before dispersing in a dull haze.

Her eyes flicked with a kaleidoscope of colors. If the eyes are the windows to the soul, then this woman had more than one soul. At first, Veri's eyes were hazel, but I swear I saw them change, going from a light blue to jade with specks of gold and back again.

"Seems we both have ended up here for the same reason," she said, looking into her glass as if she had found an answer to a long-pondered question.

"Oh," was all I could muster in response.

I didn't want to hear about her problems, and I had no intention of sharing mine. I wanted to relax, not reflect. There could be something to it, though. Maybe a story waiting to be told. That was what I hoped to find, but the sad memoirs of a dippy barfly weren't what I had in mind. However, life is life. So... I reconsidered.

"What makes you say that, Veri?"

"I was with a guy two days ago. We stopped here for a drink and a bite to eat. I told him I'd lived in this area when I was younger and began telling him about my youth. All through it, he was rolling his eyes and lookin' at the door. I went to the ladies' room, and when I returned, he was gone. The douche stuck me with a $70 check and nowhere to sleep. Since then, I've been surviving on the good graces of our pal, Dusty."

She followed this up by saying in a whisper, "To be honest with you, I think our pal is getting a bit tired of me."

Shortly after that, Dusty came by asking if I wanted another round, and against my better judgment, I said yes. When he returned with the lager, I noticed the bar had thinned out. Dusty took his two bucks and filled Veri's glass again, leaving the bottle on the counter in front of her. There was maybe one serving left in it, so I guess he just decided to let her finish it off.

I heard the chime of a clock striking midnight. Twelve long, slow peals signaling the end of a historic day in my life: the day I emancipated myself. What lies ahead who can say? I believed I had taken a long stride in the right direction, hopefully, one of discovery and happiness. Hopefully. Hopefully.

As I was lost in thought, Veri was polishing off the last of her wine. The clink of the bottle on the glass brought me back to the here and now.

"What were you thinking about?"

"When?"

"When? Just now! You know, all this time... you haven't told me your name."

"You never asked. Are you asking?"

Veri smiled but didn't ask.

"Do you believe in monsters?"

This seemed a very odd question, but I answered all the same.

"The only monsters I've ever known are the humankind." I was thinking specifically of the one I had left that morning.

"I mean monsters like you see in the movies: vampires, werewolves, the creature from the black lagoon."

"Well, I have never met such things, but who am I to say what is and what isn't."

My answer made her pause for thought, weighing and measuring it with more importance than I felt the subject deserved. It seemed such a silly question to ask or answer.

Suddenly, she blurted out, "You want to go for a ride?"

"To where?"

"There's a lake not far from here. It's a hot night, and I could go for a moonlight swim."

"A moonlight swim. What the hell, why not?"

This was certainly outside my comfort zone. If I truly wanted a new life, this would surely be an unusual start. One day ago, I wouldn't have even entertained the idea. Tonight, I was looking forward to it. A dip in a cool lake with an attractive stranger; talk about shocking the monkey. In my wildest imagining, I could not have written a better first chapter.

We both stopped at the restrooms before leaving the bar. Veri seemed anxious, if not excited to be leaving. She blew Dusty a kiss and thanked him before exiting. He didn't seem to care either way. In the lot she asked which car was mine and then ran ahead so she could have a smoke before getting in.

"I don't smoke in moving vehicles," she explained. "For some reason, it makes me dizzy."

'Good,' I thought to myself. I took half of that eight-dollar cigar I hadn't smoked with me but had no idea when I might finish. I didn't smoke as a rule and didn't want the smell of smoke in my car. That odor never seems to go away.

Veri directed me to the lake easily, even though the black of a forest night made seeing to drive a challenge. She guided me flawlessly along narrow, winding roads, my high beams glistening in the eyes of many a woodland creature as we went. Suddenly, the road widened, and the trees pulled back to expose a beautiful star-filled sky reflecting off the still surface of a large glassy pool.

"Turn to the left up here. There is a dirt road that goes down to the water's edge."

Again, Veri seemed overly excited. I, on the other hand, was not at all thrilled with the steep, rutted path she had guided me down and worried if my car would make it back up. 'Guess I'll find out when the time comes,' I said in my head while bouncing merrily along.

At the bottom, the road flattened out. There was a small parking area on the right. I pulled in slowly. I think Veri had her door open before the car came to a complete halt.

"Come on," she shouted and took off at a jog toward the lake.

When I caught up to her, she was standing on a frail wooden dock that stretched some twenty feet out into the water.

"Isn't it beautiful?"

Together, we were staring up at a star laden sky so brilliant it took the breath away. I could not believe it. I'd never seen so many stars. It was like peering into the heart of heaven. Their light colored the surface of the water in a crystalline glow, like cracked ice, tranquil and cool.

Veri turned to me and smiled.

"No moonlight, but plenty of stars."

Before I knew it, Veri stripped down and dove in. I barely saw the white of her heart-shaped behind as it dipped beneath the surface of the water. She reappeared some fifteen feet away. Her tightly curled dark hair were now straight and twisting about her neck and shoulders. As she paddled closer, I could see her eyes glowing as white as the stars above.

"You coming' in?"

My heart was beating almost too hard. I stripped down with Veri watching. A blush rose in my cheeks as I dropped my boxers on the dock and dove headlong into the pool of stars. When I came up Veri was directly in front of me, her eyes white as the water's surface.

"This is nice, isn't it?"

She put her arms around my neck. Her eyes were mesmerizing and menacing, cold and hot. I wanted to turn away, but...

"You like my eyes?"

I wanted to say they scare the crap out of me. Instead, I said "yes" because I could utter nothing else.

She kissed me softly, passionately. My heart raced, and my blood boiled. I pulled her close and kissed her harder. I stopped thinking. Nothing else mattered but the moment. I went for her neck, but after a few nice nibbles, she pulled away.

Veri made her way to the shallows and climbed out of the water onto the dock. She dried her face with my shirt and then lay back to stare at the sky. I followed after her. Climbing up onto the dock, I lay down beside her. She settled into my arms. We didn't speak; we just lay there counting the multitude of stars swirling across the indigo night.

"My name is..."

"No, don't tell me. Then I'll know you, and I don't want to know you."

I sat up on my elbows as she turned away. "But why not?"

"You want to be free. I want to be free. Knowing one another opens us up to feelings, and feelings aren't freedom. They are the monsters inside us, the vampire that sucks our life's blood, the werewolf who rips at our flesh, the creature from the black lagoon that drags us to the bottom of the lake, where we suffocate and die. I want to live, to enjoy the stars, to enjoy the moment I'm in. Don't you?"

"I do."

"Everything gets muddled and difficult when the monster is let loose."

"You say it like you know."

"Yes, I know. You know, too. I felt it in your kiss. You were enjoying the moment."

"Then why did you stop?"

"I don't want you to like me."

"But I already like you."

"You don't know me. You can't like me."

She was right. I didn't know her, and maybe I didn't want to know her. She had a dark side that ran very deep. One that might be chock full of monsters more terrifying than the one I'd just escaped. Nevertheless, I did like her. I liked her in the moment right now; who is to say whether I'd like her in the morning. Dusty became fed up with her in forty-eight hours. The guy she arrived with at the restaurant abandoned her. So, this girl was obviously damaged. I just hadn't seen it yet.

Veri sat up and gazed into my eyes. The hue of her orbs was now blue, bright blue like a warm spring sky. I never knew anyone whose eyes could change color. But then again, I'd never gone for a midnight swim, never seen so many stars, never had the guts to stand on my own two feet.

"The name of this lake is Lily Lake."

"OK."

"Have you ever heard of it?"

"No, I can't say that I have."

"There was a murder here back when I was a teenager."

That got my attention.

"My aunt and uncle had a cottage not far from where we parked."

"Did that have something to do with the murder?"

"They were murdered, and the cottage burned to the ground."

"My God, that must have been terrible!"

"I liked my aunt and uncle. I'd come up swimming all the time. Not after that, though. They never found the killer."

"Never?"

"No. It was my dad's brother. Dad argued with the cops for months; called them a bunch of stupid yokels. Didn't matter what he said. After a while, they stopped looking. I came up here a few times on my own, but it was hard. It was like they just vanished."

"You have them in your memories, so they aren't gone completely."

Veri stood up, ran to the end of the dock, and dove into the shimmering lake. I got up and followed. The water seemed colder this time, and the stars were not as bright. When I surfaced, Veri swam to me with her eyes again as white as the water, her skin as pale as a winter moon. She kissed me. This time, her lips were cold. I ran my fingers up the small of her back. Her skin was chilled. It was as if I was holding a corpse.

I pushed her back.

"Don't you like my eyes?"

"You're chilled. I think you should get out of the water."

"No. I feel free in the water."

She kissed me again. This time, it was as if she was angry, fierce and hungry. She bit me. I pushed away again. There within her white eyes flashed specks of red, like flying embers flicking on an autumn breeze.

"What's the matter? Don't you want me?"

"Yes, I want you, but you've changed. I think you should get out of the water."

"Why?"

"You're cold."

"I'm fine."

"Each time your eyes change color, a different person appears."

I swam towards the dock. I heard Veri swimming behind me, following me. When I reached the dock, I turned around. She wasn't there. I hollered for her. I dove down into the water, panicked that she might have gone under. I couldn't find her. I climbed onto the dock and yelled for her.

"Veri, where the hell are you? This isn't funny!"

I looked down the dock to where our cloths were piled. Hers were gone. I scooped up mine and dashed back to the car. She wasn't there.

The sun began to rise, stretching strands of light across the rippling water. There was no sign of Veri. I tried calling 911, but I had no signal. Finally, I gave up and went back to the diner. The place was boarded up and looked like it hadn't been open in years.

"What the hell?" I hollered. "Something is very fucking wrong!"

I continued to dial 911 while trying to get a glimpse inside this broken-down building when a police cruiser pulled into the lot.

"Hey, buddy, what are you doing?"

"Officer, thank God. I've been dialing 911 for over an hour."

"Yeah, not good cell service around here. What can I help you with, and why are you trying to get into this place?"

"I met a girl here last night, and we went for a late-night swim up in Lily Lake. I need your help. She went under, I think. I couldn't find her. She may have drowned."

"OK, calm down."

The officer pulled out his notepad.

"What time approximately did this occur?"

"Probably 5 am."

"What was the girl's name?"

"Veri, I mean Veronica, but she went by Veri."

"Veri? You mean Veronica Lyle?"

"She never told me her last name."

"Not too tall, hazel eyes, dark curly hair?"

"Yes, that's her. You know her?"

The officer flipped his notepad closed.

"Veronica Lyle died ten years ago. She was murdered along with her aunt and uncle, and then the cottage they owned on Lily Lake was burned down around them."

"No, that can't be. I met her here last night. She told me about the murder. She told me they never found the killer."

"You are right, sir. They never did. It was thought at the time that Veronica killed her aunt and uncle and then burned the cottage down around them, killing herself in the process, although her remains were never found. Her father argued against this theory, but with nothing else to go on, the case was closed."

"I don't get it. There's something wrong. I ate here last night. I had a few beers and bought a cigar. Wait, I have the other half of it in my car."

I ran to my car and began searching. I thought I'd stashed it in the center console, but it wasn't there. I checked under the seats and the glove compartment, and I even opened the trunk. It wasn't there.

"How much did you have to drink last night, sir?"

"A couple of beers, nothing really."

"Well, I don't know what happened last night, but this place hasn't been open for years. Veronica Lyle is dead, and I think you need to get some rest. I recommend the motel about four miles down on the right. The rooms are clean, and the rates are cheap. If you feel like you can't drive, I'll drive you there."

"No Officer...sorry, I didn't catch your name."

"Dusty Ramos. You take it easy, sir. And be careful driving."

The cop then put his sunglasses on and drove off.

I got into my car and just sat there. None of this made sense.

Well, I went out in search of a story, and I found a ghostly tale. Not only did I find it, I lived it, confusing as it seems. Veri, I realized, was the eraser I was searching for, replacing every thought I had yesterday. Yesterday now seemed like so long ago, and tomorrow felt like a new adventure waiting just around the next turn.

I finally decided to take the officer's suggestion and get a room at the motel. A shower and a comfortable bed sounded really good. I pulled out of the lot and headed down the road. As I came around the first bend, my heart jumped into my throat. A car, looking very much like mine, was wrapped around a tall pine tree. I pulled over. As I sat gaping, I heard a tap on my window.

"Hey, you goin' my way?"

"Veri, where the hell did you go?"

"I've been waiting here for you. So, can I get in?"

"Sure. Come around."

"I was told you were dead."

"Who said I was dead?"

"Officer Dusty Ramos."

"Dusty doesn't know anything. I have never been more alive."

"But?"

"You dropped your cigar at the lake. I picked it up for you."

"I wondered what happened to it."

"So where are we going?"

"I don't know. I guess wherever the road takes us. Isn't that what freedom is all about?"

"I believe you're right. What is your name anyway?"

I just smiled as we drove off, leaving behind all that was; in search of something new, hopefully waiting just around the bend.

The End

Little Man

How do you think you would feel at that moment, that very second when you realized your worst possible nightmare is now your grim reality? Would you feel distraught, angry, or just go numb? If this nightmare only involved you, the first inclination might be despair, but despair is much more singular, isn't it? When it involves your child, that sharp stab cuts much deeper.

A fact that might exacerbate the pain is when you make the realization that what is torturing your child is your fault. As a parent, your main purpose is to protect and keep your child safe from those things that would do it harm. Harmful, awful things can often be unforeseen or lying in wait, just needing the opportunity to wreak its havoc.

I put my son in a position where this could happen. A point his mother was quick to point out in an overture of profanity to make the devil proud. Her reaction to stressful situations always began with anger, followed by blame. I was more calculating and logical, seeking a solution rather than bathing in useless emotion. This time, however, I could not escape the perturbation. Nor could I deny my part in what had occurred to make my child ill.

Jeremy's mother, Sharna, and I met through friends while doing a photo shoot in San Francisco, where she lived. We hit it off immediately. I fell in love with her passion while she said she fell in love with my deep, sultry eyes. The truth was, in the beginning, it was all about the bedroom; I guess these were just nice ways of saying it.

Shortly after we were married, I got my big break. National Geographic hired me as a photojournalist. My first assignment sent me to New Zealand for a month to do a story on the tuatara lizard. The magazine allowed me to bring Sharna along, turning the trip into an extended honeymoon. Sharna joined me on many assignments after that until Jeremy was born. Traveling with a child just wasn't practical.

Sharna became annoyed that I would go off to so many exotic places and leave her at home with the baby. Initially she got mad when I left, but happy when I returned. Eventually, she was angry, coming and going. When Jeremy turned five, I took both of them to Hawaii. After a few weeks in paradise, Sharna seemed more content and less angry.

This carried us through about six months until I went off on another assignment that had me away for months. When I returned, Sharna greeted me with a rant of accusations and betrayal that had no basis in reality. That's when she blurted out that she had had an affair. The pain I felt at that moment, I thought, could never be surpassed. Five years later, I would learn I was very wrong.

Sharna and I split after that. Jeremy lived with his mother. He couldn't very well live with me because of my constant traveling. The court granted me the usual visitation rights: every Wednesday and every other weekend. Photo shoots in different parts of the world didn't always allow me the opportunity to fulfill this schedule, another point of angst between Sharna and me.

I would always take Jeremy for a week during the summer. This was my chance to reconnect with my son. The first few years, he came to my beach house in Malibu, but as he got older, I began taking him places. We did a week in Alaska and another in Scotland. Jeremy began to learn how to use my cameras and had a great eye for the simpler things that an adult eye too often missed.

Just after Jeremy turned ten, I received an assignment in Peru. A new Inca finding deep in the Peruvian rainforest had the boys at NG jumping for joy. The problem was that it was during my scheduled week with my son. Now ten and having a few trips under his belt, I felt this to be a great experience to share with him.

His mother vehemently disagreed. I chalked her anger up to jealousy, but she did make some valid points regarding the dangers of trekking through the rainforest. When I told my son about the trip, he pleaded with his mother to let him go, and she reluctantly agreed. I gave her every assurance that I would take great care and guaranteed no harm would come to him; famous last words and words that she would throw at me like darts later on.

My son and I arrived at the Lima airport on the last weekend of June. After a short layover, we caught a small bi-plane to the city of Iquitos in the

Northern Amazon jungle. Here, we met with two other staffers from NG who were to join us on the expedition: Cecilia Moray and Bill Wiles, two close friends and very talented journalists with whom I had shared many trips over the years. After a good night's sleep, the group met with our guides and plotted our route.

I introduced Jeremy to our troop that morning at breakfast.

"Jeremy, this is Cecilia and Bill; they will be joining us on our excursion into the jungle."

"Most happy to meet you both," he said politely as he shook their hands.

"Please call me CC. You are quite the little man, aren't you?"

"CC is right; from here on, I say we call you 'Little Man'", added Bill in his best cowboy voice.

Bill grew up in Texas and once a Texan always a Texan. He was never a cowboy, though, but he knew how to act and sound like one when he felt the need. CC was the daughter of an Army colonel and, like most Army brats, spent most of her life moving from location to location. Travel for her was just life. I don't think she could have settled down.

Jeremy was over the moon excited to be going on this great adventure and it was an adventure, one no other ten-year-old would ever experience. Now, he was 'Little Man,' a label he would wear proudly. This would be something he would brag about and remember throughout his life. In watching him, I don't believe I had ever seen him so happy. It made me happy and proud to see my son following in his father's footsteps.

He had gotten a scrapbook, and I gifted him his own camera so that he could document and save every step along the way. That morning, Jeremy ran about snapping shot after shot, not wanting to miss any part of the trip. I always felt stimulated as I ventured into a new part of the world. But to see his excitement made me feel like I did on my first assignment. My memories ran back to New Zealand. I saw the smiles on Sharna's face and felt the love we once shared. My son, being one to notice subtleties, saw the distance in my eyes and began tugging on my shirt.

"Dad, look, check out the monkeys."

"They are black-faced spider monkey's Little Man", one of our Peruvian guides explained.

Jeremy began clicking pictures, as did I. He brought me back to the present, something I thanked him for with a heartfelt hug and kiss on the head.

After approximately four hours of driving, we reached the end of the road. Now, we would hike until the sun began to set. It would take at least another twenty-four hours before we reached the ruins if we kept a good pace. There really wasn't any hurry, except that we were all very anxious to reach this new discovery. The path we had chosen to follow had well-established camping sites and we would bed down for the evening overlooking a small picturesque waterfall, which glistened beneath the colors of the most perfect sunset I'd ever seen.

My son and I sat on a stone, our cameras snapping dozens of shots as the orange and gold filtered timelessly into the thick green forest. I had photographed hundreds of sunsets in my career, but none as breathtaking as this and to share this with my son awarded me a newfound appreciation. I could see the joy in him and turned my lens. The light captured in his eyes, the dusty glow brushed upon his face, and his smile that said more than words ever could. I snapped one shot, only one, and it was perfect.

We fell asleep in our tents that night, listening to the sounds of the jungle. For Jeremy, it was a very new experience, one that both frightened and delighted him. I held him close and felt his uneasiness. When he finally dozed, so did I, only to awaken each time he would fidget, making sure that he was still safe in my arms.

Morning came much too early for me, not having gotten much sleep. Jeremy awoke full of energy, anxious to continue the journey.

"Easy, Little Man, we'll get started soon enough," Bill told him.

After a quick and less-than-satisfying breakfast, we packed up and started out again. Much of the second day's trek along this jungle path went uphill, with only an occasional dip plunging us deep into the canopy of vegetation.

Although the jungle looked in many ways similar to those forests of North America, it was much different. Each descent into darkness introduced us to new types of plant life. Inside the eternal rainforest, the air thickened with an overwhelmingly sweet smell.

"The Venus flytraps to entice insects," the guide explained ", emitted this potent aroma." These we all knew well enough to dodge.

He also advised that we should avoid the fungi growing on the trees, that these used poisons to numb their prey so that they could feed on them slowly. "These plants," he said ", can strip an animal clean to the bone."

Words we heeded with strict devotion.

The path continued to climb. We reached a long, narrow plateau late that afternoon, where we stopped to rest. One of our guides, a young Peruvian named Pallo, rushed ahead to see how far we had left to travel. Two hours later, he returned with good news and bad. We were only an hour or so away, but the route circled downward along a thin, treacherous ridge.

Somehow, we had missed this when planning our course. Now we have a problem. My counterparts and I had done extensive rock climbing; it had become a necessity of the job. However, Jeremy was much too young and had only done climbing walls at kid's birthday parties and this was no kid's party.

Our guides dug out the maps. Most of this region was uncharted territory. We reviewed the rough topographical sketches provided to us by a member of the archeological group that had made the discovery. As we searched along every contour, wanting to find an alternative route, Herberto, our senior guide, noticed something on the maps.

He, along with Bill, headed out to try to locate a cave, which cut through the mountain and led to the valley below. An hour or so later, they returned with good news. The cave circumvented the ridge and reduced but did not eliminate the danger ahead.

"If this was the rainy season," Herberto explained, "this would have water rushing through it. Now it is dry but somewhat steep and slippery. At the end, we will have to repel some fifty feet to the valley floor."

"What do you think Little Man," asked Bill, "want to learn how to repel?"

At first, Jeremy looked worried, gazing at me soulfully with the eyes of a puppy.

"Oh, Little Man. I know you can do this," said CC.

I think he was developing a little crush on CC. Her attention rose a bit of a blush in his cheeks. Jeremy straightened his back and professed, "Ya, I got this!"

I was very proud of him but still very concerned. A part of me began to think his mother was right that this was no place for a ten-year-old boy. However, by the time we dropped into the valley, Jeremy had truly earned the name Little Man, performing as well as any of us. He traversed the cave with ease and fearlessly repelled.

I saw just a slight bit of hesitation at the top, but a smile and wink from CC and he was good to go.

We made it to the ruins just after nightfall. Greeted by the team of archeologists working the site, I felt a sense of relief thinking the hardest part of the journey was over. CC and Bill introduced Little Man to the group. Jeremy was becoming unknowingly a part of their stories. I didn't let down my guard, per se, but I eased off the peddle of concern, allowing me to relax and take in the experience.

The next few days, my co-workers and I spent interviewing the scientists and photographing everything from the ground up. They explained that this section of rainforest bordered on the Cusco region of the country, a very mountainous area that shielded the valley. Climate changes caused a decline in certain plant life, exposing the ruins to the sky. A spotter plane noticed the highest pyramids and contacted the Peruvian Historical Society.

Our three-person collaboration developed a strong and comprehensive story, one that made us all feel very excited. NG loved it, too, and awarded me the cover shot. They also liked the sidebar story about Little Man, making Jeremy a minor celebrity in a very big story. I wasn't sure how to take that, but he ate it up, and I really couldn't blame him for that.

In his enthusiasm, Jeremy climbed up the side of one of the great stone structures and marched about as if he were the king of this ancient empire.

We all cheered him on, enjoying the playful display. That was until Jeremy slipped and took a tumble on a sharp piece of granite. He was fine really, just scrapes on his hand and knee; nothing a ten-year-old wouldn't get on a playground back home. CC took him to her tent, where she cleaned and bandaged the wounds. She gave him a sugar cookie from her secret stash, and he was right as rain.

On the final day, as we were packing up to start our trek back to civilization, a cluster of insects beset the campsite. The scientists identified them as a type of botfly similar to those found in Australia. Our swatting just aggravated them. Jeremy seemed to be attracting most of their attention. I had to pull him away and cover him with my raincoat to free him from the swarm. This incident made us more than happy to be heading home.

The guides for the archeologists gave us a new direction to head back, avoiding the ledge and the need to climb. It extended our trip by about half a day, but it was much less dangerous. Jeremy began feeling ill the next morning. He started complaining about pain in his hand and knee. The scrapes he had received from the fall began to look red but didn't seem to be infected.

CC cleaned and readied them again. She gave Jeremy the last of her stash of cookies, and he felt better. We reach Iquitos just in time to catch a flight to Lima. My son and I, together with CC and Bill, said our goodbyes to our guides, Pallo and Herberto, at Iquitos and then Jeremy and I said goodbye to CC and

Bill in Lima. They had an assignment in Rio and invited us to join them, but I needed to get Jeremy home.

"I will miss you, Little Man", CC told him and gave Jeremy a kiss goodbye.

Bill shook his hand and told him it was an honor to have joined him in this adventure and that he looked forward to someday sharing in another. Jeremy hugged them both and said his goodbyes with a crackle in his voice.

The flight back to San Francisco seemed much longer than it did going to Lima. It wasn't; it just felt that way. Jeremy fell asleep upon take off, but awoke suddenly complaining of pain in his hand. I pulled away the bandage and checked it. The cut was bright red and very irritated. Something odd caught my eye. I wasn't even sure if I actually saw what I believed I saw. For a split second, I thought I noticed something move beneath his skin. I watched for a minute or so and didn't see it again, so I reapplied the gauze and wrote it off as me being over-tired, my eyes playing tricks on me for lack of sleep.

Just before we landed, Jeremy complained again. This time, he began to cry. I told him we would take care of it as soon as we touched down. I gave him a

Tylenol with some water and said, "Hang in there, Little Man."

He smiled and tried to look tough. "OK, Dad."

Once we landed, I gathered our luggage and raced us across the parking lot to my car. From there, I drove straight to Mills-Peninsula Hospital. Jeremy was now screaming and crying in pain. I took him in my arms and ran into the emergency room, pleading for help. To see him crying in pain had me in tears.

The front desk nurse directed us straight into a cubical, where a doctor and nurse joined us almost immediately. When they peeled away my son's bandage, we all gasped. Numerous things were crawling beneath his skin. His scrape was now bright red and bleeding. Jeremy howled as the small lumps began burrowing up through his arm. Blood-filled maggots chewed their way to the surface in spot after spot and then tunneled back down again.

All I could think to say was, "What the hell!"

Afterward, I think my mind shut down. They rushed my son away before I could utter another sound.

"Where were you?" asked the doctor.

"Peru."

"You shouldn't have left Peru with your son having this inside him."

"I didn't know until we were on the plane."

"We need to quarantine him immediately. Nurse, contact the Bureau for Infectious Diseases."

"What do we do? How do we help my son? He is in pain."

"Yes...he is. The larvae inside him are flesh-eating. To them, he is a happy meal. This is not my field of expertise. I know someone and will get him here as quickly as possible."

"But can't you give him something for the pain?"

"I will numb the arm. That might slow down the larvae, but I don't know that for sure."

It was an hour before the specialist arrived, and he didn't speak to me; he just went straight to my son. As I waited, I realized I had to call Sharna. This was going to be ugly. I barely explained that we were at the hospital when she started ranting.

I hadn't yet told her why, but in her mind, that wasn't important. When I explained, I heard the phone hit the floor. Eventually, she said with a shaky voice, "I'll be there as quick as I can".

As soon as she arrived at the hospital, the 'I told you so's' began, flavored with just the right amount of profanity. All I cared about was our son, and if this made her feel better, I told myself, 'Let her spew'. This only served to help her and to be honest, at times, it distracted my mind from the nightmare.

I had heard about cases like this. A woman in Bolivia had parasites enter through a cut in her leg. Doctors removed the leg, hoping to stop the spread. The woman was now on life support and was not expected to live. I wasn't sure how much Sharna knew, but I didn't plan on telling her. That could only make things worse.

The doctors, led by the specialist, came to explain Jeremy's condition and the treatment options. These were few. They explained first that the scratch on his leg had no parasites in it and that the leg was safe. I exhaled a long sigh of relief and waited for the other shoe. The doctor took a long pause before delivering his assessment. I believe tears began to slip from my eyes before he even spoke.

"The larvae are a parasite that is feasting on your son's flesh," he explained with more candor than I wanted. "This is very bad."

"No Shit!" I blurted. "Tell us something we don't know?"

"We are almost positive that we have isolated these worms in his arm. Removing them is extremely difficult and painful, but we have come up with two options. The first is to freeze the arm, thus rendering the parasites dormant. Then, we operate and carefully remove them. However, we cannot be sure that the arm will come back fully or at all."

"So, you are saying he may lose his arm?" asked Sharna.

"Yes, or it may have a degree of nerve damage that may or may not be repairable. We cannot say with any certainty at this point."

"What, then, is the other option?" I asked, hoping it was better than the first.

"This is to blast the arm with radiation. This would destroy the parasites and save the arm, but the potential for long-term side effects is high."

"You mean cancer?"

"Yes, and that could manifest itself in many forms."

"So, we would exchange one flesh-eater for another?" I said facetiously.

"Shut up!" snapped Sharna. "What do you recommend doctor?"

"There are equal risks to both procedures, but I would chance to lose the arm and be done with it than give your son the possibility of a lifetime of anguish."

"Look what you've done, you asshole. He shouldn't have gone. I told you he shouldn't have gone. Why didn't you listen? Now, my baby may lose an arm, or worse. You are the most selfish bastard I have."

"We haven't much time to make this decision", interrupted the doctor.

I looked deep into Sharna's tear-soaked eyes, trying hard to see the woman I once loved. I reached out and took her hand. To my shock, she didn't pull away.

I said, "Ice the arm", and she nodded in agreement.

The doctors left without a word. A nurse came in with a release form for us both to sign. I found it hard to see through the pool of tears welling in the corners of my eyes. Large drops splashed as I signed, knowing I may have cost my son his arm. Sharna scribbled her signature beside mine and handed off the paper to the nurse.

Afterward, we sat in silence, waiting. We listened to the clock and stared out the window. I got up and paced for a while. Later, she did the same. It all seemed so surreal.

It was dark before the doctors returned with any news. They believed that the surgery went well and said they removed 100% of the larvae. Whether or not the arm would come back or whether there would be any permanent damage only time would tell.

Together, his mother and I went to Jeremy's room and sat by his bedside. Here, we both fell asleep.

It had been a long, tear-filled day dressed in pain and emotion. Exhaustion was the best feeling in an awful twenty-four hours. This was the kind of day you didn't want to remember but would never forget. A terrible day, a nightmarish day that would roll around in your mind forever. Some would turn to God, some to the bottle. I turned to Sharna and her to me, hoping that our combined strength might keep our son whole.

Jeremy remained in intensive care for many days following the surgery. Although the parasites were removed, a persistent infection with a high fever had him in and out of consciousness. Treatments to stimulate blood flow seemed to be having little impact. I contacted CC and Bill to let them know what had happened. Both found the news very upsetting. They asked me to keep them updated and said they would keep Jeremy in their thoughts.

Eventually, the fever broke, and Jeremy began to recover. Physical therapists got him up and exercising. Still, the arm wasn't responding. Jeremy seemed distant and disconnected. Now, our worry turned to his mental status. The hospital brought in a psychologist, which didn't help, at least not initially.

One afternoon following a less-than-productive session, a package arrived for Jeremy. Sharna signed for it and brought it to his bedside.

"Who is it from?" asked Jeremy.

"Someone named CC."

Jeremy looked like the light of God was upon him. His mother opened the package and stood the contents up where he could see. It was a photo of Jeremy standing on the Inca pyramid, his fist in the sky. A smile curled upon his face as he read the caption carved into the wood frame. 'Little Man conquers the Incas.' Along with it was a note from CC and Bill.

"Little Man, we are both very sorry to hear what happened to you, but we know you are strong and courageous and that you will be better soon. We look forward to sharing many adventures with you in the future, CC and Bill.

P.S. I have sent along one of my secret stash cookies to aid in your recovery, CC."

"Who is Little Man, and who is this CC?" questioned Sharna.

Jeremy took a big bite from the sugar cookie and began chattering about Peru. Suddenly, he was Little Man again, marching through the jungles of South America, fearless and determined. He asked for his scrapbook and began showing his mother all the pictures he had taken.

"I'm Little Man," he declared, "and CC is my friend. We are going to go on many great adventures when I am better."

Therapy sessions from that point on showed increasing progress. The arm slowly started to function. It became strong, and his fingers displayed more dexterity. He still had numbness in his fingertips and he tired easily, but every day showed improvement. After nearly a month, Sharna was able to take him home. His therapy would continue for many years, but he was alive, and he was whole. We couldn't ask for more than that.

Sharna and I didn't recover. Too much damage had been done along the way. We did become more civil, which I believe helped in Jeremy's healing. I started taking fewer and fewer assignments that had me away for lengths of time. Jeremy joined me on some of my easier shoots, the ones that got his mother's seal of approval.

Once he could make his own choices, Jeremy decided where he would go, which meant no more simple excursions. His skill as a photographer took him to numerous wonderful and exotic regions of the world. You could see his passion in his photos and feel his zest for life. I couldn't help but be proud to see him become so accomplished. We will never forget our trek into the rainforest, the good and the bad, the adventure of a lifetime shared in our hearts and in our minds forever.

The End

Heartbroken

Spring had come to northeast Pennsylvania in the usual way, with welcome anticipation. What remained of the white snows of winter were now small mud-stained piles of slush that would disappear by day's end. Now was the time of pastel greens beneath skies of azure and cotton candy clouds that moved as slowly as time. People removed their overcoats, replacing them with white shirtsleeves. Their brutish visages turned to broad smiles as the feeling of rebirth blossomed throughout the modest countryside.

As for me, I was in love and wore a wider smile than I ever could have imagined. So wide at times that it hurt my cheeks. I had decided that today I would ask my beautiful, beloved Becky to marry me. With that in mind, I bought a new suit, shoes, and bow tie, got myself a haircut, and shined up my spats. I went to the jewelry store and picked out the perfect ring. Yes, this was the day and although I was more than nervous, I was overwhelmed with a happiness I had never known.

I whistled a tune as I walked along the avenue, greeting each person I came upon with a 'how d' ya' do?' and 'a pleasant day, isn't it?' All felt like it was a fine day, but none had my skip in their step. That was mine and mine alone. I realized as I walked the sun-washed streets that when a man is in love, his heart beats differently: stronger, steadier, with a rhythm all its own. He stands a little straighter and walks with a sense of purpose as if life now has so much more meaning. A delightful feeling, I must say.

At the jeweler, I professed my intentions to the clerk. He shook my hand and wished me the best. Ah, yes, the best. Rebecca Odell is unquestionably the best. Even though I did not have much experience with women, I knew Becky was the finest. Her smile was as warm as any summer day and her sparkling brown eyes flecked with specks of green seemed a dream unmatched. The shape of her lips, the softness of her skin, and of her touch. She was magic, pure and simple. How could I not be in love?

After the jewelers, I stopped at the newsstand and picked up a copy of *The Scranton Truth*, something to read on the trolley ride back to Green Ridge and to my sweet Becky's house. April 9, 1909, was the date blazoned across the top of the front page. I wanted to remember that date as the finest day in my life.

Ah, it was a good day. I hadn't thought about it, but it was Good Friday, of all things. What could be finer than to ask for Becky's hand on this sacred day? She would say yes, and we would remember it and share that memory with our children and their children in the years ahead. 'So perfect,' I thought, staring out at Scranton as it passed by. I believe my smile ran away with my face at one point, grinning delightfully, lost in my vision of the future.

"You look quite dapper," said an older woman sitting across from me, breaking my trance.

"Have ya' a lady friend waitin' for ya' now?" she asked with just a bit of a brogue coloring her words. "Yes," I answered proudly. "I am surprising her today with an engagement ring."

"She'd be foolish to turn down such a delightful lookin' young man as yourself," she added.

I thanked her kindly and unfolded my paper to see what news of the world filled the headlines on this grand day.

The president of the miners' union, John L. Lewis, proclaimed there would be no strike forthcoming. His statement filled the front page, overshadowing such international news as Robert Peary planting the American flag at the North Pole and the Japanese occupation of Korea. A coal strike affected the local economy, and peoples' livelihoods hung in the balance. The Japanese in Korea or Peary's expedition had no impact on the hardworking folks of northeast PA. I didn't give a damn for any of it. These things did nothing to affect my life. Becky trumped every headline; she was all that mattered to me now and forever.

I exited the trolley with a wave and a hop, giving a little wink to the old woman who'd spoken to me earlier. She returned a gleeful smile and a shout of 'good luck', which faded as the trolley continued on its route. Only two short blocks to put my words in order, wanting everything to be right, when I knelt at Becky's feet and asked for her hand. She should remember it as a perfect day down to each word, a speech I had practiced more times than I could count.

I stopped before the church where we had met and said a quick prayer. A rush of memories passed through me, recollecting the sadness of my father's passing. It was during this difficult time that Becky's family had befriended me, knowing I now found myself alone in this world. My Mom had died when I was just a boy, and my dad was all the family I had. The Odell's kindness truly meant so much. I could not thank them enough.

However, Becky's good-hearted manner gave me life, uplifting my spirits to heights beyond any I'd experienced. Her sisters Victoria, who they called Tori, and Ginger, were equally beautiful and kind hearted, but Becky took my heart. She had a joy within her. You could see it in all she did, feel it when you were near her, and miss it when you were not. Never could I know or love another.

Her parent's house was just across the street on the corner. As I stepped from the shadow of the cross, I spied Becky on the front porch, and something inside me crumbled. Another young man had a hold of her hand in the place where I planned to do the same. I returned to the shadows, my heart in my throat, choking in pain at what my eyes could see, but wished not to believe.

"Who can this be?" My mouth turned dry as sawdust, queasiness boiled in my belly, and my legs changed to lead. I watched as the two skipped down the steps to a new-looking, black Model T. He opened the door and guided her in, then gave the car a crank before running to the driver's side and climbing behind the wheel. Tears welled in my eyes as I watched them drive off, my fingers fumbling with the ring in my hip pocket, my mind blurred with confusion.

The walk home, although only four short blocks, seemed miles. Baffled by what I had seen, I didn't have the strength to bear the weight of my heartache. Inside my front door, I collapsed into a pool of tears, my mind struggling to make sense of this unexpected turn. Had I misread all that we'd done together and said to each other over the past few months? Had she been seeing someone else and been stringing me along? She had never said the words, nor had I; it was just something understood, or so I thought.

I pulled myself up and went to the kitchen. In a cabinet above the sink, I found my father's whiskey. He'd pour a glass every night when he arrived home from work and then another before bed. He said he needed it to relax after a tough day. Dad worked in the rail yards, loading freight. It was backbreaking work, but he didn't mind. "A hard day's work is good for the soul," he would say, but I don't think he really believed it.

I worked alongside him for a short while, but it was much too hard for me. I fancied myself an artist. That didn't pay much, if at all, so I moved from job to job, earning what I could to pay for my supplies. Dad never discouraged me, always professing that if I stuck with it, I would make it in the arts one day. I did many drawings of him over the years. He would always hang the newest effort and tell me, "That's the best one yet, me boy!" I was never sure if I believed that either.

I poured a large glass of whiskey and sat down at the kitchen table. Not being one for the drink, the first swallow burned my throat, and I choked on its harsh, acidic flavor. After a brief pause, I took another, with much less discomfort. Soon enough, I'd emptied the bottle and staggered from my seat to bring out the next. Couldn't say how much I'd had when the lights went out.

The next thing I remembered was running for the toilet, where I upchucked until I passed out again. I awoke to the sound of birds singing and the dry heaves. Once I felt able, I rose to my feet and stuck my head under the faucet, running cold water over me until I couldn't stand it anymore. In the kitchen, I brewed a pot of coffee and sat down by the kitchen window, looking out at the morning. I begrudged the birds their song, wanting only quiet to ease the throbbing in my head. Troubled, I sat in silence, sullen, pain-filled, pondering what had occurred. Wanting only to go back to yesterday noon and be happy again.

I remembered denying the birds their song once before, on the day of my mother's funeral. Neighbors came to the house to pay their respects. This made me uncomfortable, and I moved to the backyard. The warble of the birds annoyed me, and I began chucking stones at the nest in a fit of anger. My father found and stopped me.

He held me tightly, saying, "This will pass me, boy. Don't let your hurt get the better of you."

Later that week, as the birds twittered to greet the morning sun, I crept through the trees. With a butcher knife clenched between my teeth, I scaled the large fir tree on the corner of the lot. A nest of young robins waiting to be fed hung from a branch halfway up. I listened to their squawking until I couldn't stomach the noise. One at a time, I lashed off their heads. Afterward, I went to my room. I could hear the angry, tortured weeping of the mother, robin, who found her children dead. Resting my head on my pillow, I cried myself to sleep.

I poured a bit of whiskey into my second cup of joe and a larger amount into my third. Soon enough, I was numb and nauseous, heading to the bathroom again. Late that afternoon, as I was lying flat-backed on the bathroom floor, I heard a knock at the door followed by the voice of Becky.

"Adam, are you in there? Adam, it's me," she yelled, sounding anxious and concerned.

I knew what she wanted to tell me it was over! That she had found another, but that we could still be friends. I wished not to hear it. I was not about to give her the satisfaction of letting me down easily. She would have to wait to rip out my heart and stomp it. Soon enough, she gave up. Once she did, I stumbled to my bedroom and passed out.

That night I walked down to Mickey's, the bar my father used to patronize. I had cleared the shelf of my father's alcohol and needed more. The bartender immediately recognized me and expressed his condolences. I thanked him and asked for a few bottles of my father's usual. He set them on the bar as I dug deep into the pockets of my overcoat to scratch out the wad of bills I had stuffed there. He peeled off the correct amount, I think, staring at me with a look of contempt. I thanked him and put the balance back in my pocket. Scooping up the bottles, I staggered out.

Outside, I pushed the bottles down into the deep pockets of my overcoat, turned up my collar to the cool, damp night air, and shuffled home. The next day, I awoke on the living room sofa, not remembering any of the night before. Church bells rang in celebration of the day at hand, Easter Sunday. I heard voices outside my window and the click of raindrops on their umbrellas as they passed by.

Sometime around midday, a knock came at my door. Again, it was Becky. I ducked down behind the drapes and peeked at her through the dirty glass. She was dressed in her Easter best with a soft pink umbrella at her side. Thinking she saw me, I pulled away and crawled into the bathroom to hide. She knocked again at the front door and then moved to the back, trying the door handles to test the locks. She moved from window to window, tapping and calling my name. I refused to answer.

When she gave up, I exhaled a deep sigh of relief. Returning to the couch, I watched her walk away until I could see her no longer. I pushed my face into the armrest and wanted to cry and then scream, "Come back, Becky, I love you. I need you. Please don't do this, please come back!" I passed out feeling alone, angry, and heartbroken.

I came to around 3 a.m. feeling something worse than awful. My stomach growled, making me realize I hadn't eaten in some time. Putting together a couple of liverwurst and onion sandwiches, I sat down at the kitchen table and stared out the window into the darkness. My reflection in the glass stared back at me in harsh disbelief. I barely recognized the wretched mess I'd become.

"She did this to me," I screamed, flinging the plate toward my image. Missing badly, the plate smashed against the window frame.

I really do not know why, but I went to my father's room and began to sort through what remained of his things. I pulled out his clothes, his shaving cup and brush, and some old magazines he kept on his nightstand. His fishing pole stood in the corner of the closet beside his tackle box. Behind that was a leather sheath that held a large hunting knife. My father stopped hunting shortly after my mother died. I never knew why. He sold his guns but kept this knife because his father had given it to him; sentimental value, I suppose.

I set the knife on the nightstand and lay down on his bed, where I fell quickly asleep. It was an arduous sleep, full of images of sadness and pain. I awoke feeling as if I hadn't slept at all. My head pulsed; the taste of liverwurst remained like a paste in my mouth. Another pot of coffee and a fifth of whiskey for breakfast, and I was back kneeling before the toilet again. Still, my head yelled, 'This is her fault; she did this to me,' as anger now replaced the pain.

Now it was time. What gave her the right to destroy me? She needed to know how she hurt me and that everything has consequences. She would learn her lesson and, by doing so, extinguish my pain. This I believed to be my only salvation.

Confront her! Confront her and show her the result of her deceit! My mind yelled this loud and harsh, flaming my fury.

The night was cool so I donned my overcoat, stuffing my father's hunting knife into the inside pocket. The scent of this spring evening filled my nostrils as I made my way along the quiet streets. Becky sang in the church choir, practicing every

Monday evening until 10 p.m. I knew her schedule well, often walking her home after practice. I would meet her in the alley, as I had so many nights before, but this time would be much different.

I waited in the shadows, listening to the choir, hearing her voice like that of an angel singing sweetly above the rest. It reminded me of the birds in the morning, how I chose to behead them so that I might suffer in silence. What used to soothe me as I waited now filled me with a rage so great it scorched my insides. I sunk into the dim, pushing my hands deep into my hip pockets. There, my fingers found the ring. The thing that once served as a symbol of my love and devotion now exists as the point of my anguish.

The music stopped. Shortly thereafter, members of the choir began to filter out, saying their goodbyes and heading off in this direction or that. Becky was always the last to exit, helping the pastor straighten up after practice. Patiently, I waited as the church emptied. Soon, no one remained in the alley. Rebecca stepped out, saying her goodnight to the good father. He locked the door behind her. Now ...she was alone.

My heart leaped at the sight of her. A part of me wanted to approach her and beg her to take me back. I wanted to cry out, 'I love you!' However, that feeling, soon squelched by the rise of anger, taking over and controlling me. I bumped against some garbage cans, feeling the knife digging into my hip.

"Who's there?" Becky asked, hearing the clatter in the shadows. I slithered back, waiting until she began to walk again. Suddenly and silently, I pounced, putting my le hand across her mouth and dragging her into the deepest, darkest spot I could find. I reached around her waist and pulled the knife from my pocket. Pinning her against the wall of a garage, I put the blade to her throat. She gazed, panic-stricken, into my eyes. I could see that she knew, and that knowing pained and confused her.

"Now you know how I feel," I said beneath my breath.

I pushed the tip of the blade against her neck. She squirmed to escape, thrashing her head about. That is when I saw the first stream of blood. She turned back to face me with a look of disbelief. I'd cut her from ear to ear. I didn't mean to. Or did I? I couldn't be sure, but when she twisted her head so suddenly, the sharp of the blade tore through her skin. Her blood poured down the front of her neck and over the lapels of her coat.

I jumped back in horror. She grabbed at my coat, trying to hold herself up. Unable to speak, her eyes pleaded for my help. She collapsed, a pool of blood spreading around her. I backed off, staring down, aghast at what I'd done. She closed her eyes and lay motionless in the damp grass. Somewhere near, a dog began to bark.

At that point, I pulled my collar up to hide my face and ran. I ran as fast as I could, faster than I had ever run before. When I stopped, I found myself near the train tracks a few blocks past my house. My lungs, my legs, and my heart ached as I bent to catch my breath. I gathered my thoughts, my hand still gripping the blood-covered knife. Scrambling into the nearby woods, I buried the knife and swept away my footprints with a switch broken from a sugar maple tree.

I went home, finding the darkest, most direct path. At home, I checked my clothing for blood spatters. Anything that did, I shoved into the coal stove, watching as they burned. I lay naked on the floor, my whiskey bottle by my side. How long could I hide what I'd done, and did I even want to? I never meant to kill her, but she had made me so angry. Now, I was not only heartbroken, I was guilt-ridden and fearful of what might happen next.

Late Tuesday came the expected pounding at my door. I knew the police would want to question me. Did I think they could prove anything? No. As far as I knew, no one had seen me. They most certainly had no evidence to link me to the murder, and besides, as far as anyone knew, I was in love with her. I would never harm her. There was nothing to paint me as a suspect; what cause could I possibly have?

When the officer told me why they were at my door, I broke down and cried. It wasn't an act; the fact that Rebecca's life had ended so tragically now became real to me. She was gone, and I was to blame. I stole the life of someone so precious. Whether they found me out or not, I would always know.

The detectives and I sat at the kitchen table while other officers searched my house, going through everything I owned.

"Mr. Welch, where were you last night around 10 p.m.?" the detective asked.

His breath smelled of cigarettes, and his probing stare made me uncomfortable. It seemed to be measuring me, weighing my appearance as well as my words. The other detective was gazing about the room, looking for anything out of place. I felt confident there was nothing here that could incriminate me.

"I was here at home," I told the detective.

I explained to them that I had been sick since the Friday before, in bed with the flu. A bug had been going around; there was no reason to doubt me.

A uniformed officer entered the kitchen holding an empty whiskey bottle and whispered something in the detective's ear.

"Mr. Welch, do you drink?" asked the detective.

"I've had a drink or two in my day, but the bottles belonged to my father," I replied. "I found them on the shelf above the sink and since I don't particularly care for whiskey, I dumped the contents down the drain and tossed the bottles in the trash."

As the officer questioned, the song of a bird distracted me. I stood and looked out my kitchen window, searching for it amongst the trees. Its song was sweet and light, and it reminded me of her. The bird flew closer to where I could see it clearly. When it did, I grabbed a cup from the counter and pitched it, just missing the winged pest.

"That should quiet it!" I exclaimed and returned to my seat.

"Sorry, birds annoy me," I growled.

Both detectives seemed surprised, exchanging glances of concern at my sudden actions.

"Why so angry at the song of a bird?" questioned the first detective.

"Maybe Miss Odell's voice angered you. I understand she had a beautiful voice," stated the second, who was now standing beside me.

"I would never hurt Becky. I just don't like birds", I answered defensively.

After a lengthy exchange of questions and answers, and once the other policemen had completed their search, the detective stood and thanked me for my cooperation. Just as he was about to exit, the detective asked again, "Are you positive you have not left this house since Friday, Mr. Welch?"

Again, I reiterated that I had not, but at the same time, realized my lie. 'Could these local cops be smart enough to figure it out?' I asked myself. Even if they did, it still doesn't make me a killer, just a drunk and a liar. Now, I'd just have to wait and see.

Later that evening I cleaned myself up and went to the Odell house to give condolences. Mr. Odell greeted me at the door and thanked me for stopping by but declined my entrance.

"The family is in a state of shock, my boy. Best you wait to pay your respects when things have settled," he told me. I shook his hand as a single tear escaped him, falling from his eyes that looked so deeply wounded.

The police released the body to the family four days later. The family had the viewing for Becky in the sitting room of the family's home. Many people came to pay their respects to a beautiful girl with a magical spirit. I came in composed as a Christian hypocrite, shaking hands and sharing hugs. After I had said my prayers over the woman I loved, Becky's sisters approached me, accompanied by the young man who had destroyed my dreams.

I shared hugs with both girls before they stepped back and introduced the gentleman. He was a handsome man with dark eyes and wavy brown hair. Slightly taller than I first perceived, but that, of course, was from a distance and through distressful eyes.

"Adam, this is our cousin Harold Hunter," said Tori. "Harry has been in town for Easter. Becky very much wanted you to meet him."

He reached out to shake my hand, but I was too stunned to move.

"Are you alright, my good man?" he asked, seeing the color drain from my face. "Rebecca did nothing but speak of you. You know she loved you very much," he added. Still, I said nothing.

'What had I done? My god, what had I done?' my mind screamed, drowning out every voice in the room.

Finally, I shook his hand and politely excused myself.

"I do apologize; I am still a bit under the weather. This awfulness has taken me aback. I hope you will please forgive me. It is nice to meet you, unfortunate that it must be under the worst of circumstances."

I exited the home and began walking the seven or so miles to the Scranton police station, where I intended to turn myself in for Becky's murder. I'd only walked two blocks before I realized I was not alone. The detective who had questioned me in my home was now walking along side me. Behind him were two uniformed officers. I stopped and gazed down Sanderson Avenue, knowing my life as I knew it was over.

"Mr. Welch," began the detective, "I'm arresting you for the murder of Rebecca Odell, but I think you know that, don't you?"

I nodded but did not respond. The two officers, who had been trailing us, stepped up and took me by the arms, handcuffed me, and led me into a waiting police car. I stared out the window, watching the same scene of Scranton that I had seen on Good Friday, heading in the opposite direction.

The detectives had done their jobs well. After questioning the bartender at Mickey's, they discovered I had lied about being home with the flu. The bartender told them that I was wearing an overcoat and smelled of whisky and vomit. They also found a witness who saw someone in an overcoat run into the woods near the tracks the night of the murder. There, they found the bloodstained knife. Still, this evidence could only be considered circumstantial, but it was enough for an arrest.

I admitted what I had done and why. After a lengthy trial and despite public outcry to condemn me to death for my crime, the court found me to be mentally incompetent. The judge declared it to be 'a crime of passion,' remanding me to a mental institution for the criminally insane.

Now, I spend my days staring out through bars of my own making. Bars cast in false assumption and self-doubt, of presumption, without ever attempting to know the truth. I realize that my weakness brought me to this place and that my hurt had gotten the better of me despite my father's warning.

The hospital allows me to use my sketchpad and crayons, and I draw every day. Some days, I draw images of my father; other days, of Becky. However, hers I find somewhat distorted, not at all, as I remember her to be: dark images of desperation, which are so unsettling. I think I shall not draw her much more. I believe I found another subject, more to my liking.

My only visitor is the caseworker, Miss Juliet Riles. She is very sweet and kind of heart, with the most beautiful blue eyes. She has made the time here seem almost pleasant. I hope that if I ever leave this place, she and I can possibly become something more than patient and counselor. What light through yonder window breaks? It seems my smile has found its place again.

The End

The Shallow Hours

I awoke to the fragrance of honeysuckle clinging to the hush of a summer morning. The scent... seemed to be one with the fog that slowly withered beneath the rising of the sun. I sat up in my bed, dazed and gazing through my window and into the garden. The appearance of a cardinal and then two gave me cause to wonder just how true the old rhyme is, that says, 'If a cardinal appears, an angel is near.'

"What angels would be looking in on me?" I questioned.

My loved ones have been gone for so long, and I have moved so often. How would they even know where I live? Perhaps... angels follow the heart... so no matter where you are, they always know. It is a hopeful thought, a pleasant thought, but more likely, this is just the wishful thinking of an old man.

A rap on the door had me thinking other foolish thoughts. Possibly, my angels had learned to knock. Maybe they wanted to stop by, have a glass of sweet tea, and share a memory as we watch the grass grow on this profoundly hot summer day. With the second knock, it occurred to me that it was much too early for company. Who would come to my door with the sunrise? Who indeed!

Neither family or friends since I had few of one and none of the other; so, who might this stranger be and why?

A part of me didn't want to know, but of course, my curiosity and concern got the better of me. This must be important, yet still I meandered, in no rush to receive bad news if it was bad news being delivered. Having any news delivered in the shallow hours of the morning seemed most inappropriate. These days I realize that propriety has lost its place in common society. No one seems to give a damn about anyone or anything beyond themselves and their own wants and needs. So why should this impingement be of any surprise?

It could just be the time of day that has me perplexed and unnerved, but I prefer not to be that grumpy old man who desires solitude. Too often, too old leads to too alone and that person I do not wish to become. With this in mind, I will greet this uninvited intrusion with at least half a smile and cautious eye, saving my ire until I am more informed.

If nothing else I will get to talk to someone, something I haven't done in days. I believe my last conversation was with Mrs. Kilmer across the way, searching for her lost cat, or with Jackson, the mail carrier. Oh, wait, Jackson retired some months ago, in the fall, I believe. I remember him saying he did not wish to endure another winter. Understandable; I do not relish the thought myself. Too many aches and pains creep in during the cold winter months, but it is much more comfortable on the warm days.

Therefore, I will be gracious, if not glad, for whoever it might be and whatever cause that brings them to my door. Once they have gone, I can go back to my day, perhaps prune the flowers or fill the bird feeders so as to attract more angels to the yard.

A nap in the afternoon and one cold beer at sunset while watching the firefly's dot and dash between the evergreens.

One cold beer, that is all, just enough to quench my thirst and relax as night falls when memories crawl back in to torment me. If only I could have stopped at one. Some lessons we learn the hard way. The consequences of these harsh teachings we often take to our graves and so shall I, I suppose.

I could still smell the honeysuckle and hear the song of the cardinals as I made my way to the foyer. Sunlight poured in through every window and filled the corners of every room. For a moment, I couldn't tell if the creaking I heard with every footstep was the floorboards or my bones.

No matter; I will have to live with either. Such is age.

Upon reaching the front door, I realized the knocking was rhythmless, a morbid tapping, pale and pedantic. I had never heard anyone knock this way, making this morning's disruption stranger still.

"Who is it?" I asked, but no one answered.

Thinking I had not been heard, I asked again with slightly more inflection and bravado.

"Who is it!?"

Still, no voice answered back. This was ruder and more annoying than disturbing. Reluctantly, I undid the latch and deadbolt. As I twisted the knob, the tapping ceased. I opened the door cautiously, just a crack at first so I might peek, prepared to shun the unwanted. A sliver of light struck my eye allowing me only a faint image, a dark silhouette pressed against the white.

Opening the door wide, streams of sun filled the foyer, much as it had filled every windowed room.

I do not recall much going forward. I do believe I began to dream, at first, of my friend Chance Landers. We had been boyhood chums, growing up together in the old neighborhood. I learned to drive from his father, and his mother made wonderful pies. He went into the service after high school and fought in Korea while I went off to college. Chance was the best man at my wedding, a glorious day full of laughter and memories. We drifted apart after that for no other reason than life taking its course.

I began to think of my wife, Charlotte. I recalled the scent of her hair when we lay sleeping. Just then, it dawned on me; it was honeysuckle. Oh, she was so angry that it rained on our wedding day and the day the twins were born. It rained that terrible night of the car accident when I lost them all, and many years later, on the day we buried Chance.

For a moment, my heart felt the pain of all of these all at once...and

then it didn't.

There, in the shallow hours of a summer morning, I came face to face, toe to toe, with that which had weighed upon my heart for much too many years. Self-reproach is a faceless foe that, if harbored, will age you faster than the days. Clocks cannot be rewound nor deeds undone. Appreciating this grim axiom in itself is a daunting task. Relinquishing those burdens, those companions you have lived with for the better part of a lifetime is harder still.

I'd like to think that I shed a tear, but I don't recall that I did... as I bid to put to rest the onus of a half century.

"Why had it come to my door on this day?" I asked in anger, as if it needed a reason or invitation.

For ten years, I begged for forgiveness; for forty, I begged to forget.

Now, with the scent of the honeysuckle and the twitter of my angels, my strength is gone, as is my pain, at one with the fog that slowly withers with the rising of the sun.

The End

"Brown House"

To tell this story, I must go back in time. Back through the years, back to my childhood growing up in Scranton's south side. The sixties filled the history pages with changes, many that didn't reach my town so quickly. Scranton's better days were behind it. Seeing properties in disrepair were becoming commonplace and although I was very young, I noticed.

Our neighborhood, however, showed no signs of decline. It sat proudly, a sanctuary in a swirling world, insulated and detached. At least, that's how it was for me, but again, I was young. Well-tailored lawns, finely kept houses, and a nice car in every driveway, that was my street and every street for blocks in all directions.

Until one day, while playing with friends in the schoolyard of Franklin D. Roosevelt Elementary School, one was pointed out to me, along with a warning: never go near that house.

Of course, as a child and one who tended to do the opposite of what I was advised, my curiosity became piqued. I crept to the edge of the playground and stared down upon this house, measuring it. My older sister, Dori, had issued the warning. Her words followed me, as did she, repeating her alert and adding that she'd tell Mom if I went near it.

Once we reached the fence that surrounded the playground, Dori stopped. Together, we gazed down on that brown house, wondering what dangers lived behind those walls.

I asked my sister why we should never go near it.

She said, "The old ladies who live there are witches."

I was so young I still trusted in Santa Claus. Believing in witches... well, that was easy. I'd just seen The Wizard of Oz for the first time, which just strengthened my imagination's ability to accept without proof. I didn't question it, not for a second. The question was: was I going to do anything, as in anything stupid?

Undoubtedly, something stupid was not my intention. Looking down at that old brown shingled structure, with its decrepit porch, and the whole lot surrounded by a rusted wrought iron fence, I appreciated that it was not someplace I wished to go near. The entanglement of weeds and shrubs that spilled over, through, and around that failing fence invoked the image of a vast spider web ready to entrap any child who ventured too close.

I hated spiders, and the feeling of webs made my skin crawl, yet there was something pulling me. My sister clutched my arm, her eyes still gazing at the house in horror. I felt her nails pierce my skin, responding with the typical, "Ouch," before pulling away.

"What was that for?" I asked, rubbing my arm.

"The old lady is staring back at us."

I looked back toward the house. My eyes locked on the deep, sunken, bloodshot glare of a gray-haired termagant whose glower was nothing short of terrifying. She must have seen us looking at the house, and I felt sure she was not happy about it. Suddenly she disappeared from the window. The front door of brown house creaked open. Before the old woman could step onto her rickety porch, we were hoofing it, our Keds slapping the asphalt, running faster than I ever did.

Have you ever noticed that when you want to get somewhere in a hurry, it seems to get farther away? We were only two short blocks from our house, but it took forever to get there. Having been born with cerebral palsy, my gate was off, and I stumbled multiple times, although I did keep up with my sister, either compelled by fear or she was holding back so that I wouldn't lag too far behind.

We reached the front porch of our house, gasping for air and laughing like two fools.

"Don't tell mom."

"Tell mom what?" she answered with a smile.

Sometimes, sisters can be cool.

My left leg was hurting from the run; then again, it always hurt. I'd always been in pain from my handicap. I just considered it normal because I didn't know any different. My leg hurt, my ankle hurt, and even my left arm hurt sometimes, but I never said anything or told anyone. I didn't see the point. To me, it was just the way it was. Everyone deals with something. This was my something.

Dori and I went inside to get a drink, still giggling about our race home and breathing heavily.

"What have you two been up to?" asked my mother, who greeted us in the kitchen.

"Nothing, just running. We need a drink," Dori answered.

My mother looked at her with a suspicious eye. She knew we were up to something. She always knew but brushed it off as kids being kids.

My sister pulled two cups from the cabinet, filled each with tap water, and handed one to me.

"Dori, remember your brother isn't…" Mom stopped herself. "Just watch out for him."

"Yes, Mom."

"She doesn't have to watch out for me, Mom. I'm okay. I even kept up with her this time."

"He did, mom. He really did."

"Well, that's good. Maybe your leg is getting stronger. You two go get cleaned up. Dinner will be on the table soon."

Walking away, I asked, "Is Dad home yet?"

"No, he is still painting at the Angelo's. He'll be home soon, though. He has your brother, Charlie, with him, so not too long, I expect. Go wash your hands now."

"Okay. I want to tell him about our race."

I stopped in the hallway as I heard Dori whispering to my mother.

"I heard that!" I shouted.

"No, you didn't," Dori shouted back. I could hear the smile in her voice.

She was right, I; I didn't. But I felt good about myself. Whatever the truth might be, it couldn't change the way I felt.

My father came home just as Mom put dinner on the table. My brother, Charlie, had paint on his hands, so Mom took him to the bathroom to scrub it off. All I could think was, 'He is not going to like that!' I'd been there. Mom never spared the scrub brush. It was worse if you fussed. She would get it all off, along with some skin.

When they returned to the kitchen, Charlie looked a little pink. Guess he had some paint on his face and neck. He sat down between my father and my sister, Denise. You could see a touch of tears in his eyes, but he didn't make a sound.

Our older siblings, John, Kerry, and Ema, had moved out. That meant more room at the table. John joined the service, Kerry married and was raising her own family, and Ema, the free spirit of the bunch, a true child of the sixties, had headed for New York City to become a part of the cultural upheaval. I wished I was old enough to do the same, but unfortunately, I was born too late. She was living her best life, and you had to admire her for that.

"Charles, would you like a piece of chicken?" asked Mom.

She only used our full names if you did something wrong. That told me he fussed. Unlike the rest of us, Charlie would fuss again and again. He just wouldn't learn. Also, we weren't having chicken for dinner, but we called everything chicken; otherwise, Charlie wouldn't eat.

"Hey, Dad, I kept up with Dori running home from the schoolyard today."

"Well, that's great!"

"He did, Dad. He was with me every step of the way." Dad glanced at Mom, who smiled and nodded.

"We are proud of you, Tommy."

Dad didn't say it; he never said it. I didn't notice it then, but in time I would.

By the time we finished eating, my brother had forgotten about the scrubbing and asked if he could go out to play in the yard. I went with him while the girls helped Mom with the dishes. Dad took Andy out of the highchair, cleaned him up, and brought him into the living room.

I probably shouldn't have, but I told Charlie about the witches of brown house. I told him I wanted to go down there, but he was quick to say, "I'll tell ma, I'll tell ma!"

Needless to say, I assured him I wouldn't and never shared a secret with him again.

That night, before falling asleep, I gazed through my window. I could see brown house glowing in the soft white of the moon. For a moment I thought I saw one of the sisters standing in the window and, I swear, she was staring back at me. A chill ran through me as I stuffed my head beneath the pillow, the image of that gray-weathered face etched upon my brain.

I fought sleep, fearing my dreams would be nightmares. I wasn't wrong.

I saw myself crawling through the thorny brush and stinkweed that surrounded that wretched place. Dented paint cans hung from bowed branches, spilling black and red ooze that trickled in crooked streams through the undergrowth. Even in my dreams, I wanted to turn away but couldn't. I saw the old woman in the window, her red eyes and black teeth pushing out from her pruned face.

Suddenly, a second witch materialized out of thin air, another weird sister. She extended her long, thin fingers through the rusted fence, attempting to grab hold of me. With her dirty, yellow fingernails, she caught my shirt and let out a menacing cackle. The crone pulled me towards her, with me frantically slapping at her arm in a futile attempt to break free. My screams of terror went unheard as I fought in vain for my freedom.

My shoulders became wedged between the fence spindles. That's when my shirt gave way, tearing apart at the seams. I jerked from her grasp, becoming airborne to hide in the clouds. The last thing I remember was the high-pitched shrieks of the sisters, distraught by my escape.

I awoke in a cold sweat, screaming for help. My mother came in and settled me with a hug.

"It was just a bad dream, Tommy. Nothing that can hurt you. Just a bad dream."

Mom rested my head upon my pillow and tucked the blanket under my chin. I had endured night terrors since I was in the hospital with the first surgery on my leg. She knew well how to quiet me. One soft kiss on the forehead, and I was asleep, drifting into soft, pleasant dreams.

From that night forward, the dominant subject of my dreams was the witches of brown house. What I noticed was that these were much more real than most I had experienced. I found myself flying to escape and then waking up feeling suffocated. I think it was the dreams and not my sister's warning that kept me away from that place. Yet, that pull I had felt remained like a needy, unsatisfied desire.

August turned to September and that meant back to school. It also meant I had an upcoming birthday. I didn't like school. Even elementary school sucked. Some of the kids were good about my handicap, some weren't, and some could be downright cruel. It certainly didn't help that I was a dopey kid, awkward, and sometimes just downright stupid.

Usually, the bullying stopped after a few weeks, except for a choice few that never let up. Sometimes, I wanted to cry; other times, I'd get so angry I just wanted to punch them. I never fought at school, but I had a couple of skirmishes after school. That never helped anything.

My birthday was fun. Mom made a cake with thick chocolate icing, and my siblings sang Happy Birthday. That was the good part of a big family. There was always a crowd for celebrations. I got a Hot Wheels set with two cars and a track. Charlie and I set it up in the hallway and we played with it until it was bedtime. That night my dreams were not of witches but of parties and racing down that bright orange track to victory.

Later that month, just as the autumn colors began to paint the leaves, there was a news report that a young boy had gone missing. I didn't know the boy and couldn't remember his name. He was a sixth grader. They didn't talk to the little kids like me.

I do recall it was a frightening time for both children and parents, wondering, worrying, and praying. The gossip around the playground was that the witches were responsible for his disappearance and that they'd dropped him in the witches' well.

Although I'd never laid eyes upon it myself, rumor said it lay hidden beneath the dense shrubs that grew so out of control they folded over one another. Only the most fearless of fools would fight through the twisted web of branches to discover its whereabouts.

Compelled by the reports, the police went to the property. The ear-piercing shrieks of the two sisters, refusing them access, could be heard throughout the neighborhood. It took hours to calm them down enough to allow the officers onto the property. They had to sickle their way through the brush to reach the well.

Kids and adults alike lined the avenue to see if the police discovered anything. They did, but it wasn't the fault of the sisters.

Three boys came forward and admitted what happened. They dared their friend to go onto the property, sneak onto the back porch, and steal the broom the old ladies used to chase away the neighborhood children when they got too close to the yard. The boys said that there friend got frightened when he heard one of the old women shouting from an upstairs window. They also said they saw their friend climb into the well through a gap in the hedge.

When the two sisters came out yelling and screaming, they took off.

Also, they said they thought their friend would escape once the coast was clear. When he didn't, they were afraid to say anything because they thought they'd get into trouble. In my neighborhood, if a kid got into trouble, they got smacked. Not just spanked but thoroughly smacked. We all feared it but knew that most of the time, we deserved it. These kids abandoned their friend and then didn't tell anyone for days. What do you think they got?

What we found out much later was that the missing boy climbed into the well, which was about fifteen feet deep. The big problem wasn't the depth of the well or that it was crumbling. The floor of the well gave way. Our neighborhood and many throughout the city were overmined. Old coal mine tunnels crisscrossed beneath the surface. Subsidence had collapsed houses and backyards. When the boy fell, he slid down a mineshaft another twenty feet or more.

I don't know the exact truth of the information about the condition of the boy, but what I heard made me want to vomit. He had many broken bones, his body lay covered in coal dust, and he'd been gnawed by rats, apparently while he was still alive, as there were signs of shielding wounds. After the body was removed from the well, the city had it sealed so that there could never be a reoccurrence.

At least, that's what they thought.

Somehow, the sisters reopened that well.

Halloween came around, and with it, much chillier temperatures. The brightly colored leaves became brown and brittle, gathering in untidy piles and swirling with the slightest breeze. Jack-o-lanterns decorated every house except one. Brown house needed no seasonal decorations. A gray haze clung to it like a perpetual shadow. Even on the few sunny days we had, the place looked bound in darkness.

Mom heard that some kids in the neighborhood had been caught throwing stones at brown house. Of course, she didn't call it that. She made it clear that we were never to go near that house or show any ill will towards those women.

"My god, they must feel terrorized! Having people smashing their windows and harassing them for no reason. What is the matter with these children? What are their parents teaching them?"

We assured her that we had nothing to do with it and never would. I looked at Charlie, who looked like he was about to spill about what I had told him months before, but he didn't. Instead, he blamed one of the neighbor's kids who he said he saw throw a bottle onto the porch.

Mom became visibly upset and scolded Charlie for being even remotely involved. Dad came in just as Mom was finishing her lecture. He stood in the

foyer, quiet, conflicted, wanting to interject, but he knew better than to interrupt my mom. Once she shooed us away, Dad sat down on the couch beside my mother.

We all went to our rooms at mom's demand, but that didn't mean we couldn't hear our parent's conversation. Dad had stopped at Morton's Store to pick up some groceries on the way home from work. The two sisters were in there giving Rick Morton a hard time. After the women left, Dad said Rick described them as pure evil, the meanest people he had ever met.

"My delivery boy won't go near the place. He told me they tried to lock him in the kitchen the last time he dropped off their bags. He said there was a skinned cat hanging above the sink with its eyes popped out. Also, the news article about the missing boy was on the kitchen table. They'd cut it out. Said it looked like they were saving it."

Dad said to Mom, "Maybe the kids in the neighborhood are tormenting them. That could be, but Rick says they are crazy, and he thinks they are dangerous! Now, I don't know them, but I think we should be concerned about what these women might do, concerned about the kids."

"Either way, the point is the same: for the kids to steer clear of that house for their own sakes. No one should be tossing stones at someone else's house. If our children are there, they can be accused even if they hadn't participated, and you know Charlie knows how to find trouble."

That would be the last we would hear about it for quite a while. Winter roared in just after Thanksgiving and didn't let up until early April. Along with the snow and cold, winter brought many changes. The youngest child, Andy, no longer used the highchair. He'd grown enough that he got a seat at the table, but never next to Charlie, who liked to pick on him. I mean, Charlie pestered all of us, but Andy got the worst of it. Also, everything didn't have to be called chicken for Charlie anymore. He finally realized we'd been lying to him all along.

I was in the midst of a growth spurt, getting taller, but not much heavier. Mom took me for therapy a couple of times a week. Afterward, we would enjoy chocolate malteds at a soda fountain across from the hospital. My body was getting healthier, but the doctor felt the first operation hadn't done enough to fix my leg, which was twisted inward. He felt a second operation was needed, but he wanted to wait a while until I was stronger.

Spring burst forth and, with the help of a golden sun, dried up the last remains of winter. This meant recess out in the playground, which was as joyful as it was hectic. Children churning about in a fun-fueled frenzy: running, chasing, skipping, and flipping as if the schoolyard was a massive trampoline. When two kids crashed into each other, a pushing match ensued, and that led to punches being thrown.

Unfortunately for me, it was Charlie who'd slammed full speed into a third grader. I knew the kid. He was as unpleasant as he was stupid. He knocked my brother to the ground, and in turn, I knocked him to the ground. It wasn't the first time I'd stuck up for my little brother. Too often, he brought it on himself. It didn't matter; he was my brother, and I would protect him. Teachers broke it up quickly enough before Stupid and I started swinging. We all ended up in the principal's office, where we received a scolding before being sent back to class.

What hung in the background of all this happiness? The shadow of brown house. All the kids knew about it and only talked about it in whispers. Looking down on it from the playground you could see the forsythia beginning to bloom. It flowered ever so briefly, choked by the prevailing weeds. Soon, it would be as dead as everything else that bordered that eyesore.

Our school let out for summer break around mid-June. You have never seen so many ecstatic children. The last day of school was like Christmas, the Fourth of July, and your birthday wrapped up with a sunny bow. There were probably a few kids that liked school. I didn't know them, so really, in my world, they didn't exist.

On the weekend after July fourth, Dad stayed home instead of working, which was rare. He either went to work at the factory or did house painting for someone. Dad did whatever he could to put food on the table. That morning, he made us breakfast and later cut the grass before tending to his tomato plants. In the afternoon, he drove Mom to the hair salon, even though it was only a few blocks away, within walking distance. I think Dad liked to drive her there. He probably considered it alone time, even though one or some of us always wanted to go along for the ride. Sunday, he would take one of us to Romeo's Pies & Pastries to pick up dessert for Sunday dinner. That was our treat.

When he came home from dropping Mom off, Dad turned on the ball game and settled in to relax for a while. Somewhere around the 7th inning, the phone rang. Dad answered, said OK three times, and hung up. He then called down the hall for me.

"Tommy, take a run down to the salon. I'm going to give you some money to bring to your mom. Guess she's a little short. Now, listen to me, don't stop for anyone, and don't let anyone know you have this, all right?" He paused and then leaned over to look me straight in the eyes then said, "Do you understand?"

"Yes, Dad."

He straightened up. "I'll watch Andy. Do you know where Charlie is?"

"No, Dad. He went out to play with Graham. He might be at his house or at the playground."

"All right. You get going. If you see him, send him home."

"Okay."

With that, I headed out the door and down the street. During my walk I saw no one; not a neighbor, not even a car passed me as I went. I could hear kids at play in the schoolyard. I could hear dogs barking and birds singing, but not a soul did I see. I couldn't help but wonder why, but I only wondered for a moment. Things like that didn't plague the thoughts of a kid my age.

What caught my attention was brown house. I didn't have to walk right past it, but I was in closer proximity than was comfortable. I made sure that I stayed as far away as I could and sped my pace to a brisk walk just short of a run. Still, it pulled at me like a magnet. The draw was something I couldn't explain. The closer I came the more it tugged. Not enough, though, as I held my course and completed my task.

Mom thanked me and told me to tell Dad to pick her up at four. I said I would and off I went, somewhat fearful of the journey home, feeling the strength of the draw, worrying I could not resist. After leaving my mother at the salon, I began to notice more activity around me. Cars sped by on Main Avenue, there was a woman pushing a stroller further up on O'Hearn Street, and I heard music and laughter resonating from the beer garden across from the salon.

I crossed O'Hearn Street in the hope that I might get a glimpse of the activities inside this place that seemed so full of joy. The windows along the street side were too high for me to see inside. However, the back door was open. I slipped around the corner and onto the small concrete step leading up to the door to peek inside. It stunk of beer and cigarettes.

The amber ceiling lights glinted off the assorted bottles on the shelf behind the bar. The bartender, a tall, thin man with a handlebar mustache, was wiping the countertop and sharing a laugh with two men seated at the nearest end of the island. Two women were dancing in the middle of the room, their skirts flaring high above the knee, while a young black-haired man in a pin-striped shirt played piano. Another group of people at the far end of the barroom were singing and toasting with large mugs of golden ale. A thin veil of smoke hung about the lights.

"Thomas!" I heard someone shout from behind me.

I recognized that voice and that tone immediately. It was sharp and laced with judgment. My mother must have seen me through the window of the salon. 'Oh no,' was all I could think.

"Get away from there and go home! That is no place for you."

I dropped my head and turned away. "Yes, mom."

I began to walk, thinking, 'That looked like so much fun. Can't wait till I'm old enough.'

I walked on, not realizing where my steps were leading, still lost in the thoughts of what I'd just seen, particularly the women dancing. I found it exciting in a way I'd never felt before. Lost in dreams and sensations, when I finally looked up, there, sunk deep in the gray and green overgrown hedges, hid brown house. And I was in the alley directly behind it.

For some reason, my fear went away, replaced by a gnawing curiosity to see what lay behind the hedgerow. I moved closer, stealthily dodging the loose piles of dog shit that dotted the court. 'Gross,' I thought to myself. 'People need to pick up after their pets.'

I heard the screech of a cat before seeing a mangy-looking calico moving through the underbrush. The hiss of a second cat made me look harder into the thicket. That's when I saw one of the sisters belly up to the stone wall, which I assumed surrounded the well. She pushed something in, but I couldn't see what. It landed with a thud as the old woman coughed out a sinister laugh and then headed back to the house.

'I thought the well had been sealed' was the first thing that ran through my mind.

My youthful curiosity raced, needing to know what she'd tossed into that hole with such malicious delight. Better judgment must have returned home without me because I sure didn't have it. I pushed open the black rusty gate, which was no easy task. The twisted weeds had climbed up and around the posts and were not letting go without a fight. I managed to create just enough of a gap to get my narrow body through.

A cat slithered between my legs. Not the calico, another one, orange and white striped with a cut off tail. It hissed as it got behind me, curling in and out between the gate spindles. I moved forward, my eyes flashing between the back door and the well. The air thickened as the prevailing sun turned gray. Nothing about this was good, yet I continued forward, compelled by something beyond curiosity.

Shoving past the last hedge, I reached the stone wall, crouching down behind it. My eyes affixed on the back porch and door, ensuring I hadn't been seen before I rose up to look over into the pit. Just as I stood, another cat, this one black with a white chest, leaped from the entangled branches and onto the stone wall. I noticed that it had an eye missing and a scar beneath its chin. It hissed, then jumped away.

My neighbor, Trudy, had told me that cats guarded the houses of witches. She said that the witches could see through the eyes of the cat, and that is how they knew when someone was stirring outside. She warned me not to go near brown house much the same as my sister did.

Right now, I was thinking, 'I should have listened to them.'

Trudy, as we talked that day, some months earlier, had given me something. She said, "Just in case."

"Tommy, this is a dog whistle, the type of whistle only a dog can hear. My dad works at the Army Depot. He told me they use them to train military dogs. I have two, and I am giving one to you."

"If you can't hear it, Trudy, how do you know it works?"

Trudy blew her whistle. I heard nothing, but the dogs started barking. She blew it again. Dogs began appearing, running towards us from all directions. I got nervous, but not Trudy. She smiled and reached into her hip pocket. She began to feed each dog that arrived treats, even tossing a few to me to feed them. Before I knew it, we were in a frenzy of wagging tails.

Trudy said, "The witches and their cats don't like dogs. Keep it with you. If you get in trouble, blow the whistle. The dogs will come running. My bedroom looks out towards brown house. If I see the dogs, I'll know you are in there and will get help."

"I have no intention of going near there, Trudy."

"Maybe, but for some reason, I get a feeling you will." I didn't fully understand, but I was beginning to.

My attention turned from the one-eyed cat and to what lay in the well. Shock ran through me, aghast at what I saw. It was my brother, Charlie, tied up with a rag in his mouth. He stared up at me, trying to yell.

That's when I felt it, the hot, foul breath of someone behind me. It was one of the sisters. She grabbed me before I could move. I struggled to get free, but she was much stronger. She lifted me up and ran into the house through a basement door tucked away beneath the thickets. The door slammed, and we were in the dark. She tossed me to the floor. I hit my head and felt dazed as I listened to the sound of metal clanging.

The spark of a match in the darkness brought me to my feet. The old hag lit a candle, then lit three more before blowing out the match with a poof. I found myself locked in a cage with a dirt floor and cobwebs hanging thick between the beams above my head. The sister gazed at me over the candle's flame. She had one eye and a deep scar running down her chin to her neck.

"We've got you now, haven't we?" she rasped.

A door opened. Through it, a smoldering light poured down upon a crumbling set of stairs. The soft click of footsteps filled the quiet. The sister I'd seen through the window, who haunted my dreams, appeared as if she'd been there all along.

"We've got you now, little Tommy," said the second sister. "Yes, we do."

"You know me?"

"I've been in your dreams, Tommy. I've been in your head. Oh, how sweet it was when your mommy kissed your little forehead and tucked you in. You'll never know that again."

Her tone went from sing-song to nasty. Even through the poor candlelight, I could see the shine of her black teeth, her eyes bright with satisfaction at her catch.

"Can we eat him, sister?"

"No, Marta, not this one. This one has a true heart."

My mind somehow stayed steady and clear. That's not to say I was without fear. I was terrified. But I felt like I could handle it. First, I needed to free myself. Couldn't do anything if I didn't manage that. Then I had to save my brother. If my nightmares taught me anything, it was that there was always a way out. However, flying was definitely not an option.

I remembered the gift Trudy gave me during our conversation about this place, when she advised me to stay away. What the witch said let me know the choice wasn't mine, no matter the warnings. Maybe Trudy saw this day coming. She seemed to have a sense for things concealed beyond the norm.

A dog whistle now became my best weapon. I slid my hand into my pocket, digging deep until my fingers touched the thin metal gadget that I carried with me unused for so long. If the witches saw it, they'd surely confiscate it, so I had to be cautious. My timing had to be perfect.

"True heart? What does that mean?" I asked.

I wanted to get them talking and, maybe by doing so, get them to turn on each other. Marta seemed subservient to her sister, Black Teeth. That can lead to animosity between siblings. Coming from a big family, you find this out early. Not one of us was ever the boss, at least not yet in our young lives.

"What does true heart mean, and why do you have black teeth?"

Marta started to answer but was hastily pushed aside by her sister.

"Marta, hush!"

Marta cowered in the corner. "Yes, Giselle." "Boy, you sure treat her badly," I noted.

"Shut your damn mouth, boy."

"Giselle knows, and she'll feed you to the cats."

"Marta, I told you to be quiet. Now, go set up the bowls and unsheathe the athame. We'll be needing to bloodlet this one."

"So, you're not going to answer my questions," I prodded.

Giselle glided towards me and put her face against the cage. The smell of rot came with her. She licked her lips with a muddy tongue, long, brown, and thin. The white of her eyes was as red as Dad's tomatoes.

"You bastard child, I'll answer your questions, so you can piss yourself in fear at the thought of what awaits you."

I could see I was agitating her and didn't see any reason to stop.

"Still haven't heard an answer. My mom says people who use curse words are stupid."

"I'm gonna make your mommy cry before this day is out!"

Gisselle moved to the worktable to see if Marta had set up the bowls correctly and scolded her when she found them improperly positioned.

"How many times do I have to tell you? You gotta get them straight. That was sister Clara's mistake. Where are the eyes of the Siamese that I had you remove?"

"Oh, where did I put them?"

"Remember, sister," scowled Giselle. "We need those."

"I think I kept them in the cold room, sister."

"Well, get them. We'll need to stir them into the worm brew when it boils."

Giselle lifted a large wriggling night crawler out of one bowl and dropped it into a pot, while sister Marta picked up a candle and scurried into a room beneath the steps. The entire time, I was clinging to the whistle in my pocket and thinking, all the while my eyes scanning the room, determining the best way out, not only from the cage but from the house.

Giselle looked over her shoulder and began to explain, "A true heart is one that is loyal, faithful, and knows love. It is strong and happy despite the pain it endures. Although I loathe all these qualities, they are necessary ingredients for the waking spell. I've been patient, waiting for the day to trap you so that I could take from you what I needed. Your brother was the final bit of bait I required. You've been his protector, and for that, you will suffer."

Giselle paused, concentrating as she took the knife (she called, the athame) in her hand and turned to me. The reflection of the candle's flame danced upon its blade.

"I understand, though. I protected Clara, but she was reckless, never listening.

Once she tastes your blood, she'll come back to us. Then, together, my sisters and

I will feast upon you."

"Well, thank you for saying all those nice things about me," I responded, painting each word with a tone of sarcasm.

Giselle turned her back to me again and continued her work. She took a match and lit a pot of something on the bench where Marta had lined up the bowls. It flashed bright orange and then settled into a steady flame. This gave me the opportunity to determine whether I could slip my skinny frame between the bars. A plan was forming in my head. Soon, it would be time to try.

I didn't know if Marta had locked the cellar door behind us when she brought me in and tossed me to the floor. I was banking that she forgot just like she forgot how to arrange the bowls. Giselle began to chant. I assumed it was part of the spell she and Marta were conjuring.

The bars of the cage door were tight and immobile, but the two in the center to the right were loose. Before starting my escape, I removed the whistle from my pocket, put it to my lips, and blew. Afterward, I stooped down to get my head through the bars, then turned my shoulders. Despite being thin, I got stuck about my ribs. My eyes were steadfastly affixed on the balding head of Giselle, who was busy with her chemistry.

"Marta, where are you with the cat's eyes?"

"There are four sets of eyes in here. Not sure which is which."

"I marked the container with an S. You saw me do it, you daffy crow."

"I got them."

"Good. Bring out some rotted toadstool when you're coming. I need the mold to mix with the worms."

"Yes, sister."

Emptying my lungs of all air, I finally managed to squeeze my torso through the bars. My hips then came through easily. I was out just as Marta exited the cold room. Seeing me outside the cage, she screamed, "Sister!" When she did, I blew the whistle again.

"This is delicate work, crow! What are you blaring about?"

The barking of dogs descending on brown house came from all directions. I lipped that whistle one more time for good measure. You could hear them on the porches and scratching at the doors, including the basement door. I wished I had treats and was a bit concerned that I didn't.

"He's escaped, sister!"

Giselle turned around as I rushed past her and seized the vessel with the orange flame.

"Grab the little bastard, Marta!"

I ducked under her lung and tossed the fire onto Marta's back. Her dry, ragged clothes burst into flames. She staggered, her arms swinging wildly as I sprinted for the basement door to let in the dogs. Giselle screamed in horror at the sight of her sister burning. The dogs headed straight for Giselle, who did her best to fight them off. She reached the stairs with the dogs biting at her calves.

Racing to the well to free my brother, I saw smoke billowing from the basement door, followed by tongues of orange flame. A firestorm climbed the outside walls of the back of the house. The dog pack poured out in a rush, scratching their way through the weeds and twisting their bodies through the fence balusters.

There was the sound of children yelling coming from the front of the house. I could hear it as I pushed through the thicket to the well. Chris was tied to a rope that was knotted at the other end of a tree branch. I untied it and put the rope around my waist. Placing my feet firmly against the stone wall, I began pulling. It must have been an adrenaline rush because I brought him up easily.

As I unbound him, I heard Giselle's shriek and glass breaking. The web of hedges was now sparking, as was the back porch. As Charlie and I pushed our way out of the yard and into the back alley we heard the sound of approaching sirens. Looking back at brown house, I saw something that chilled me to the bone. It was the ghostly impression of another younger sister. Her cold eyes gazed down at me with deep disdain. I watched as the blaze gathered up and swallowed her.

My brother and I raced to the front of the house. There we found a line of kids pelting Giselle with stones. Among them were the neighborhood dogs howling as the flame rose higher.

The police and fire trucks arrived just as we did. The sight of them sent the last witch, black teeth Giselle, into a frenzy. As great plumes of fire exploded through the upstairs windows, Giselle ran inside, into a spray of flames. She ran to her death as the house collapsed into a pile of burning timbers. When this happened, the line of kids cheered. A glorious end to that wretched place and one most deserved.

The police called my parents to the scene. We explained to all of them what had happened. Mom and Dad were fit to be tied, and not all of it was directed at the witches. As they berated us for our part in the events of the day, I spied Trudy in the background, standing between her sister, Liz, and brother, Jimmy. They'd come with her to stone the house.

I smiled at her. That was me saying 'thank you.' If it wasn't for Trudy this day could have ended very differently. I heard her mother yell for them to come inside, and they were gone. How Trudy knew, I don't know, and I never asked. Truthfully, we weren't that close before she gave me the whistle, and we weren't close after; friendly and neighborly, but nothing beyond that. I will never forget what she did for me, though, keeping it our secret to this day.

Now that we are older, the memory needs to be brought out and put to rest. The fact that I took two or maybe three lives, still bothers me. I never truly knew what I saw that day standing in the upstairs window. That image I kept quiet about. Only two bodies were pulled from the rubble, Giselle and

Marta. I believe the third, Clara, would never be found as she was no longer a corporeal entity, trapped in the sleeping spell and somehow beyond the laws of this world.

Still, the images invade my dreams from time to time, but I no longer fly away. Astral projection, I've discovered, is easier for children as doubt is something that is learned with time. Now, I stand my ground and deal with it, clear and steady. I do, however, miss simply believing.

Don't you?

The End

"Help Wanted"

'Help wanted, phone 733 284-7623'

That was the entire notice that fell from between the folds of the diner menu. Someone had torn it from the newspaper and forgotten about it. This scrap of paper could have been days old or even weeks old. I really couldn't tell how long it had been there, and honestly, I really didn't care. I needed a job, and my need was as unspecific as this one-line ad ripped from the classifieds.

It seemed plain enough to me that this job matched my skill set perfectly since I had few, and it asked for none. There is no need for references and no mention of a background check; that's good, but that might come after the interview. Actually, there wasn't a mention of an interview; not much to go on. All I could do-was make the call and hope for the best.

I sipped the last of my coffee, wiping the traces of coffee grounds from my lips. The diner's coffee was the absolute worst, but it was one dollar for all you could drink, so I was getting my money's worth.

"Fill me up again, Sadie. I need to make a phone call," I told the waitress before stepping away from my seat and heading down the narrow aisle to answer this strangely ambiguous ad.

The Silver Plate Diner had an old-style phone booth at the end of the counter.

You know, the type with the polished wood bi-fold door and wooden bench seat.

The little space always smelled bad, but you could never really identify the odor. I dug my last two bits out of my hip pocket and sat down. Dropping my quarter in the slot, I dialed the number, and waited. After four rings, a recorded voice answered, "If you are calling about the ad for help wanted, leave a number at the beep, and we will call you back."

I gave the number of the phone booth and hung up the receiver. As I did, I noticed a book of matches on the floor at my feet. I picked it up and shoved it into my hip pocket. Don't know why I bothered since I didn't smoke. Maybe I just needed to have something besides lint in my pocket. Sometimes, it feels better to have something for your fingers to touch, even if that something is just a book of matches.

As I stood up, the phone rang. The suddenness of it startled me a bit, having gotten lost in my thoughts of empty pockets. I lifted the receiver. Before I could say hello, a voice asked, "Are you the person who just called this number?" "Yes," I replied.

"Come to this address at noon today. 7 Dark Region Road."

Before I could ask a question, and I had a few, the line disconnected. Now, it was up to me. How badly did I need a job? Answer: very. I had a short list of things I wouldn't do for money. Prostituting myself and murder sat at the top. I might sell an organ if the price was right, but that is a different story entirely.

I returned to my seat at the counter and took a sip of my coffee while deeply considering going to this meeting. I had no idea where Dark Region Road was; just the name made me nervous. There really was only one thing I was completely sure of, and that would finally sway my decision. I hadn't a penny to my name.

Up to this point, I'd chosen every wrong path for my life to go down. In school, I partied when I should have been studying. In life, I gambled when I should have been cautious and complained when I should have kept quiet. The only thing I had in abundance was debt, and that wasn't something that could be wished away. If there was an opportunity to be had, I needed to take it, or things were never going to change.

I had paid for my coffee with my last buck, and my old Valiant was running on fumes. I couldn't be sure I'd make it to wherever this meeting was, but I had run out of options. Just as I made up my mind, the postman came into the diner, delivering the daily stack of bills.

"Hey buddy, hold up a second," I shouted.

"Yes sir; what can I do for you," the mail carrier politely replied.

"Would you happen to know where 7 Dark Region Road is?"

He told me it wasn't that far away, but also explained that the road was unpaved and not someplace you want to get stuck. He gave me directions along with a menacing good luck and then headed on his way. With no gas, no money, and no choice, I said so long to Sadie and headed off to meet the unknown.

The mailman's directions were spot on; however, his description of the road fell well short. He described it as unpaved; he should have said barely used. Two tire tracks cutting throw a thickening twist of nightshade and buckthorn. Only fifty yards in, the canopy of trees began choking off the light from the late morning sun. At one-hundred yards, I flipped on the headlights, as the area became black and damp as a cave.

At two-hundred yards, my headlights fell upon a large number seven carved into the mossy bark of an old oak tree. Beyond this stood the broken remains of a wrought iron gate, rusted and wrangled with a creeping black-leafed vine. My beams exposed the outline of a long driveway buried beneath the encroaching vegetation. I climbed out of my car and pushed the gate back as far as it would go so that I could get my car past without adding a new scratch to the collection.

Slowly, I maneuvered my old bucket of bolts down the narrow passage, the sound of branches and thorns scraping away what little paint remained on this less-than-classic automobile. The road began bending to the left and then came to an abrupt end in the shadow of a huge gray Victorian-style house. I sat gaping at this crumbling structure protruding through the abysmal forest. Nothing about this seemed good, nothing at all.

My car clunked and gasped to a halt, leaving me with two options: get out and run like hell, or take my chances and do what I came here to do. "Ah, what the hell, what's the worst that could happen?" I said aloud so my ears could hear the words and then stepped out of my car and onto the porch.

The thick stench of rotting vegetation surrounded the house like a blanket. I could feel it clinging to my arms and on the back of my neck as I stood at the front door, reconsidering my decision. Before I could knock (or run), the door creaked open, releasing a musty, dry air that easily displaced the scent of decay.

I yelled, "Hello!" but got no answer in return. Again, I yelled, "Hello!" adding, "I'm here for my 12 o'clock appointment." Still, there was no reply. Swallowing a deep, dry swallow, I stuck my head inside.

Just beyond a drift of dust, which seemed to move rhythmically through the foyer, shined a dim light. I walked towards the light, thinking to myself, 'Is that really what you should be thinking at this moment?' The light did not seem that far away, but the walk felt eternal. Heaviness, like the weight of an anchor, dragged at me, making each step a challenge. When I reached my destination, I just wanted to sit, but there were no chairs. The only piece of furniture in this grim vacant space was a small round piecrust table propping up a slender white candle pressed firmly into waxed over chamber stick.

The light of the flame brightened as I approached it, illuminating the room with a hazy white glow. I panned the room. It was a library, with shelves reaching from floor to ceiling on every wall, each teeming with books and not a space between them.

A thin lace of cobwebs hanging from the ceiling and a gathering of dust bunnies accumulating in the corners were the only failings in an otherwise tidy room.

'Quite a bit better maintained than the rest of the property,' I thought.

Again, I hollered, "Hello!" figuring someone had to have lit the candle, but again there was no response. The silence became louder, more noticeable, as it took on a presence all its own. There was something else in the quietude, an energy drawing at me. I could not be sure, but I believed it to be the books. This magnet had pulled at more before.

There was a time when I was quite the ravenous reader, losing myself in the words of Poe, Dostoyevsky, Melville, and Wells. I would live in their worlds, joining their characters in great adventures and in their sorrows. I immersed myself in the pages. If I came across a flawed plot or grammatical error, I enjoyed the story more, feeling that it made the thoughts more real, more lifelike: flawed as life is flawed. To presume a writer should be perfect is as preposterous as assuming we know how life should be and that one's path is the only path; again, flawed.

I took the candle and waded about the room, gazing at endless lines of books, some large and thick and some no more than novelettes. It took me a moment or two before I realized that none had titles, only names running down the spine. I perceived this to be the author but recognized not even one. Having read thousands of books, I expected to see someone familiar. To know none of these writers was very strange.

The light flickered as I noticed a book with a red cover bearing no name. I glanced quickly about to see if any other blank volume existed, but saw none. I took it from the shelf and returned it to the table in the middle of the room. Setting the candle down, I cradled the book in my left hand and flipped open the cover. As I did, a note fell from between the pages. I set the book on the table and unfolded the note.

It read simply, "Welcome to the Library of Souls; thank you, but your services are no longer required."

The sound of the front door shutting shook me to my core. When the library door swung closed, the light from the candle withered and then extinguished. Now, darkness surrounded me, one so deep it hurt my eyes to look upon it. I headed in the direction of the door, but found no handle. Stumbling about, I felt for a crease, but found none. There was no door frame, no hinges, no seams to indicate where the opening should have been.

Frightened, I thought, 'What trap have I stepped into? What poor choice is this?

What wrong turn have I made now?'

I hollered for help but knew immediately that it was pointless. Reaching into my pants pocket, I found the book of matches. I struck two at once, searching through the amber glow of the area where I remembered entering. There were only shelves of books disappearing into black at the edges of the sparse light. As the match light faded, I struck two more and made my way back to the table in the hope I could find the candle, but there was no candle.

There, on that old dusty table, I found only the nameless book with the red cover.

The match light nipped my fingertips, and I dropped them to the floor. I lit another. What I saw next distressed me more than anything that had gone before. This untitled book now bore a name etched in black along its spine, a name I knew. This name was mine.

I thought I should be terrified, but I wasn't as I turned the pages to see the description of my conception, my birth, my first day of school, and so on. As one match elapsed, I lit another and then another so that I might read of joyous Christmases gone by and drunken, delightful New Year celebrations. Fireworks filled Fourth of July's, my first kiss, the birth of my first child and its passing, my broken leg, my broken heart, and the self-destructive route of my decline, all penned in prose like none I had ever read.

Long lost memories floated on long-bending rivers in my mind and then poured like waterfalls onto the pale pages, words woven with such talent and flare to make even my mundane and misspent life sound intriguing. My heart ached with the highs and lows, and not a moment left untold. I felt myself begin to fade with the shrinking light of the final match until I became a name on a shelf beside endless volumes ~~of~~ gathering dust in the darkness. A story lived~~,~~ but never read. A single edition, original in its own way, and most certainly, flawed.

"Hello, is there anyone here? I have come about the ad for 'Help Wanted.'"

The End

"An Autumn Tale"

September began, feeling much the same as July and August, hot and muggy without even the relief of a trickle of rain. There were, however, some noticeable changes, as the atmosphere rearranges its particulars. Mixed in among the bright green forests that blanket every hillside, there appears the occasional tree whose leaves just cannot wait to change. Usually, this anxious ent. is a sugar maple or white ash, two types of trees that simply love to show off their true colors.

These are the doormen arriving early to usher in the season. To some, this is exciting, to see the orange of fall. Others see only winter on the heels of a season that steals away the warmth and sun-blessed days they love, barbeques and fireworks, swimming pools, and ocean views; such are the glories of summer. These doormen allow autumn to enter and, in doing so, remind summer to take its glories and go.

As the month wanes and the October winds descend, the landscape and sky become a kaleidoscope of color. The musky scent of the season rides upon the breezes, an intoxicating fragrance that saturates the fall. However, for as brilliant and beautiful as these might be they are but a colorful distraction, concealing the thin gray wisps that drift amidst the gloaming. We see them as cobwebbed clouds twisting in the fading light, but in truth, they are so much more than what our eyes perceive.

The ghostly host of autumn has such a subtle color we overlook its presence as it gathers in the shadows. The blazing hues fill our eyes, and they ignore such forms disguised betwixt the garish delight that brightens every leaf. Gliding swiftly beyond the glow of the street light, this necromancer searches for disembodied souls, inviting them to join it as it races across the calendar to the destine day.

We think, as people so often do, that we know all there is to know; our splendid conceit is almost laughable. Still there are those who realize what stuff resides beyond our sight, but even they don't really know the truth. If they did, I believe they would be less accepting of the mysteries cloaked and conspiring within the umbra.

I have a friend who speaks to the dead, and she believes that what they say is legitimate. Truth is what you perceive it to be and what you can prove, of course. Nevertheless, a spirit will tell you any number of things, usually from their point of view; unfortunately, that does not make it true. The story I am about to share, I cannot prove nor will I attempt, but this autumn tale most certainly changed my mind about what is and what might be.

As I walked a damp black street one night, beneath a grainy strand of light, I caught a glimpse of something slithering in the dim. Startled, I stepped back a stride, rubbed my palms into my eyes, and bent my neck to find a better point of view. Gazing into the swirling shroud, a puff of smoke, like a piece of cloud, rose up and rushed hastily away.

I felt a chill, a bitter cold and smelled the stench of something old, musty as dead leaves after a November rain. Unsure of what I thought I saw, I chased this smoke for several blocks, until I found myself at the cemetery gates.

I stretched my chin above the balustrade; my eyes affixed on the gathering gray glowing beneath the rising of the moon. The last specks of sunset dripped away, blood-red stains lingered eerily, and my heart began to pound in sonorous beats. A figure dressed in tattered threads, carrying a severed head, approached me through a fracture in the fog.

Aghast... I compelled my legs to run, but instead, they followed one by one the dank and crackling path of listing leaves. Face to face, I found myself chatting with this cloven skull, who said his name was Henri Laguille. Now I am just a normal man, not one to believe in fairy tales or creatures that hide beneath my bed. Nevertheless, here I am with this, conversing in a creeping mist with a head dangling from a specter's grip.

Henri, it seemed, was quite insane, asking for Dr. Gabriel Beaurieux, insistent that they had spoken just seconds past. I assured him I was all that was there except our friend, this ghastly ghoul who seemed to be connected to the gloom.

"Nonsense!" he said, "he is the undead come to shake the witches from their chaste vows. He took me from a basket weaved, by an orphaned child left to feed on scraps swept from a café floor."

"Dr. Beaurieux, I heard him speak. He called my name after the guillotine had punished me for my wicked ways. I killed the child for a slice of meat, defiled her corpse without remorse, and then buried her beneath the painted trees. Her blood now drips from the tips of these autumn leaves.

This being said, look about my friend; there are many things concealed... in the charnel field."

My eyes careened about the lot until they fell upon my family's plot, where the souls of those I loved presided. A man in a grimy pinstriped suit with spats and rats about his feet lit a long and badly bent cigar. He leaned an elbow on the broken stone and then cocked a finger toward the unknown, a blank spot left un-carved on the family slab.

I knew this space was meant for me, but I wasn't leaving that easily. Not being dead I felt the choice was mine. Other spirits came to call. They fell like rain from every cloud until there were no clouds left in the sky. Henri was smiling like a fool, his face aglow in the harvest moon as these phantoms began to swing and sway.

An orchestra crawled up from the mud with electric guitars and a man on drums who looked strangely like the Beatle's Ringo Starr. His hair hung straight, his eyes but holes, his drums encrusted with rust and mold; still, he never missed a beat. My feet, too, began to move; even the specter got in the groove, breaking out a twist on Don Pablo's crypt, a tomb in ruin yet still under lock and key.

Of all the things I thought I'd never see.

"What day is this?" I heard me yell as I watched the Broadway show from hell, prancing across the graveyard in a frenzied fit.

Henri responded with delight, "October 31st, a hallowed night, party time for those souls that just can't leave".

"But I'm not dead. Should I concede... that this is where I ought to be?"

"Your day will come," a dark voice said, slow and deep. "I'll arrive just when the time is ripe. Your type is oh so readily deceived."

Right then, I felt my neck hairs curl and decided to vacate this swirl of madness, twirling out before my eyes. I backed away until my heels clicked, thinking, 'This is what I get for sticking my nose where it does not belong.' Midnight rang from the church bell towers on old Main Street as the dark devoured every living thing left in its way.

I ran swiftly from the falling leaves, returning to the damp black streets where I first spied the sight of something strange. No time had passed, no moment spent.

My curiosity I will long regret. However, there are still some questions left unsaid.

Did Henri ever find Dr. Beaurieux? Did he ever locate his arms, and legs; who or what is trapped within Don Pablo's tomb? Will the specter ever learn to dance? Shall the witches discover true romance, and who was the man smoking the bent cigar? Sometimes, you know, a cigar is just a cigar.

In the morning, the world had turned brown. The brightly colored leaves were gone, and charcoal skies resided everywhere. The doormen had let something in with thinning hair and wrinkled skin and then abandoned their posts like cowards often do. November winds blow cold and shrill, stripping every tree until the hillsides wear a beggar's coat at best.

The ghostly host arrives in splendor, vibrant as the fire and amber, but leaves a wretched semblance wandering in the cold. He is merely a drab, deceitful passerby with a wicked bit of twinkle in his eye. Neither sad nor in the least remorseful, his glorious days are but a fistful. What he came to do is what he leaves behind.

Now.... this story is my point of view, an autumn tale that might be true, but truth is not a gift one just receives. When a spirit tells you something else, try to decide what you have seen and felt. And, if you notice a bit of cloud, perhaps you might want to think about those things that possibly exist amidst the gloom. Remember, never lose your head, or you might end up with the undead, dancing beneath the ashen light.... of a harvest moon.

The End

"Wyndam"

The small town of Wyndam never had much going on. It was nowhere near any big city, had little nightlife, and almost no crime. It sat along a small, serene river named after the Lakota Indians. The Lakoquanee or 'Quiet River' seemed to set the mood for the entire town, calm and meandering with little worries beyond the weather. When sunshine and warmth blessed this little town, tourists came to Wyndam, a place they could go to escape the rat race, sit back, and relax.

The town had a meager, but spreading reputation for fine dining and quaint B & B's in a setting so quiet you could hear a pin drop. The worst criminal act ever committed was when some tourist ran out on their tab at one of the local restaurants. The town's economy relied heavily on tourism, so the locals considered this a crime punishable by death. Money here, like anywhere, people held in high regard, possibly not as high as in the city, but when your pockets are light, every dollar has meaning.

I myself discovered the place completely by accident. I had become increasingly fed up with the city, so one Saturday morning, I hopped in my old 74' Mercury Montego and went for a ride. Writing in the city, I realized, was like napping on a wood chipper: noisy, irritating, and completely unproductive. New York, if I could make it there, I must have sacrificed what little morals I had left. Seems everyone wanted something to help you climb the ladder of success. When you wouldn't bend over for them, they forgot about you, like you never existed at all.

Ah, my old Montego: midnight blue with silver metal flake. So many memories rushed back into my head as I sped along, enjoying the scenery. My father had given it to me just after high school, and the first thing I did was burn the seat when a seed popped, exploding the end of the joint I was smoking. This would be the only blemish in an otherwise pristine interior.

I had my first sexual experience in this car. Becky Dunes, my first true girlfriend, would slide across the big bench seat and cuddle up to me as I drove. One night, as I was taking her home, she slid her hand between my legs. We hadn't gone there in our relationship yet. Delightfully surprised by her sudden fondling had me swerving the car all over the road.

"Relax," she whispered, taking a little nibble of my ear.

She unzipped my pants and began to stroke me. As she did, I struggled to concentrate. My foot eased off the accelerator, and I swear my eyes went blurry as the blood rushed quickly south. I realized the blood rushing away from my brain again, reliving the memory to the point that my car swerved, invading an already occupied lane. Car horns blared as I pulled the car back into my own lane, mouthing my apologies to the driver next to me, who mouthed back, "What the hell, asshole?"

Thoughts of Becky floated in and out of my head often. We split when she joined the service, and I headed off to college. I heard from her every now and then. She even threatened to come to visit me in the city, but never did. She hated New York, the crowds, and that big city attitude as if they knew everything and the rest of the planet was just struggling to figure it out.

Becky wasn't the type to tolerate arrogance, not even from me, and I could be an arrogant prick when I wanted to be.

The last time we had spoken, she had returned to our hometown, having completed two tours in Western Europe. She'd gotten a job working part-time as an EMT stationed at the old number fifteen hose company, not ten minutes from my family's farm. I'd said something stupid to her during our last phone call; some adolescent sexual innuendo bullshit. She called me a jerk and hung up. I tried to call her a few days later, intent on apologizing, but she wasn't having it. That may have been the last straw, sending me on this road trip, wanting to clear my head of everything, including Becky.

After nearly three-hundred and fifty miles of straight driving, my oil light began to blink; at three-hundred and seventy-five miles, it stayed on for good. I guess taking a spur-of-the-moment road trip in a twenty-one-year-old car with over 150,000 miles on it may not have been the best idea. I knew I needed to get it checked, but I could not remember when I had passed a gas station last. I'd let the highway behind to follow the back roads through the countryside, wanting to see truer Americana and fewer billboards. This put me on a windy road in the middle of nowhere, begging my car not to disappoint me before I could find help.

Another growing problem occurred to me. The beautiful so blue skies, which had accompanied me throughout my trip, were being replaced by a dark and ominous gray. I felt the wind gusting strong enough to shake my car. Considering the weight of this old rattletrap, I knew immediately this was no ordinary wind. I'd grown up in the Midwest and learned to recognize the telltale signs of severe storms a.k.a. twisters, and this began to have all the markings.

Maybe it was me. I had survived two tornados and now big winds and strong thunderstorms freaked me out. Having seen the devastation firsthand, I believed my fears to be amply justified. I questioned whether this part of Pennsylvania had ever experienced a twister. I had never heard of one touching down in this part of the country, so it seemed doubtful, but I was no meteorologist and could only go by what I knew, and what I knew was that this didn't look good!

A short, but surprising pelting of hail increased my anxiety, not having experienced a hailstorm in many years. Again, a more common occurrence if you live in Kansas, 'but Toto, we're not in Kansas anymore' I said to myself. Hail, too, can be a precursor to a tornado. My senses now on high alert, I believed I had driven into something even worse than life in New York City.

As the road pitched around a turn to the left, I caught my first glimpse of a small town squeezed between a green-sloping hillside and a seemingly motionless river. At this point, I began a gradual and winding descent into my past. The wind continued to rise and fall, gusting stronger with every turn. I fully expected to hear storm sirens screaming as I entered the town and was stunned when I did not.

Every fiber of my being, wished to check the oil, gas up and run. However, trying to outrun a twister rarely works, particularly when you are not tremendously sure what direction it's coming from. I rolled into a Gulf station with the car's engine ticking frantically. Even if I chose to run, I don't think my car would have cooperated.

"Well, that doesn't sound good, my friend," said the station attendant as he approached my car.

I was completely content to pump my own gas when the man asked how much I wanted and started doing it for me. Can't remember the last time I'd been in a full-service station, but who was I to complain?

"Fill it up!" I told him and then reached beneath the dash and popped the hood. Moving to the front of the car, I slid my fingers beneath the hood to locate and release the latch.

"Oh, don't chew' go botherin' with that, sir, I'll get it for yuz,'" said the man.

"Why get cher' hands all dirty? Mine is already greased up, and yuz' should problee' let her cool down a bit anyways."

Knowing little to nothing about cars, I couldn't help but agree. "Soooo, where exactly am I?" I asked the man who had finished pumping my gas and was now wiping down my car's dipstick with a filthy rag.

"Yer' in Wyndam, Pennsylvania; Population three-hundred and fifty, give or take," he replied.

"Three-hundred and fifty, ya' say?" I repeated somewhat facetiously.

"Give or take," he repeated.

After a brief pause, he said, "Yer' at least two quarts low, mister. Whatja' really need is an oil change. I can do that for yuz' if yuz' got about an hour ta' wait?"

Looking around, I saw very few people on the streets, but those that were seemed very unconcerned by the approaching storm. Maybe it was because the wind was still very gusty, with moments of calm balancing the periods of swirling draughts, lulling them into a false sense of security. The bending and twisting of the trees told me a much different story, however.

"Are there storm cellars or shelters in this town?" I asked the gas station attendant.

"Nah. What would we need them fer'?" he answered and asked.

"You got a big storm coming in," I told him. "You ever have a tornado come through here?"

"Tornado? Hell no!" he scoffed.

"You see the way those trees are twisting and the cloud formations hanging over that clearing across the river?" I asked him while pointing to the thick black cumulonimbus clouds in the distance.

"Yeah, so what of it? We've had wind here before. 'Sides nothin' noteworthy ever happens in this town, outside a' some petty theft and maybe some drunken disorderly. That last part's usually me on a Friday night, and today is Saturday," the man replied.

I thought about this for a moment and couldn't stop myself from laughing.

"You a weatherman or somethin'?" the attendant questioned.

"No," I answered, still gazing at the black and gray storm front heading straight towards them. "But I've lived through two tornadoes, and I've seen this all before. Hail, heavy winds, twisting trees, and clouds as black as the Ace of Spades."

"If you say so, mister," the man answered, still not believing there was any impending danger.

"You wantta' pull yer' car into the garage for that oil change or just have me add two cans a' ten w-forty so you can get on yer' way. Don't wantta' get caught in another tornado after all. Do ya' now?" the attendant said with a snicker.

Whether the man wanted to believe it or not, the wind was picking up, and the lulls, well, there weren't any lulls. It had become an increasingly steady whirlwind, sending to flight anything that wasn't nailed down. Loose branches, leaves, newspapers, and trash swirled in a dynamic dance up and down Main Street. Even with this happening all around him, this man showed little to no concern, believing wholeheartedly that a tornado could never come through Wyndam.

Inside the greasy little shop attached to the garage, an old transistor radio crackled. The voice of Patsy Cline cut through the static, singing 'Crazy,' a song I remember my mom playing ad nauseam when I was a kid. She loved Patsy Cline, and 'Crazy' was her all-time favorite song. As a youngster, I hated Patsy. Hearing one singer all the time can do that to a person, but now that I am older, I realize she was a very talented singer with a tremendous voice. How many present-day female artists could you say that about and really believe it?

The attendant came in wiping his hands with the same filthy rag he'd wiped off the dipstick with. Just as he did, the voice of Patsy Cline stopped. The radio began to squeal with a loud, ear-piercing din. The voice of a man proclaiming a warning from the National Weather Service filled the little room.

"This Is an Emergency," the voice shouted. **"Tornado Alerts are in effect for the following counties."**

The list was short, but too long to listen to and much too late for the town of Wyndam. I stood staring out the window, across the river to where the storm fronts collided. I watched as the funnel formed, ripping a wide path of destruction as it bore down on this sleepy little town.

"Where is the nearest basement," I hollered to the attendant.

The man didn't answer. He just stood gaping at the fabulous fury of nature, which was about to tear his town down.

I grabbed his arm and asked again, shouting at the top of my lungs, trying to be heard over the roar of the wind. The man pulled away in disbelief. Frightened, he backed off, crashing into a rack of oil cans and falling to the floor. I knelt down, grabbed him by the shoulders, and shook him in the hope of breaking the trance he'd fallen under.

"We need to get out of here. We have to get below ground, or we're going to die. Do you understand?" I shouted.

Finally, the attendant snapped out of it. The fear in his eyes frightened something inside me. I knew the feeling. I'd experienced it when I was ten as a twister destroyed our family's farm. I saw the funnel coming, the noise louder than anything imaginable. I felt like my limbs would be torn off. My father swept me into his arms and ran across the field and into the storm cellar, with the twister biting at his back. My mother and brother struggled to get the doors shut behind us. I remember landing hard on the floor as my father threw me down and went to help them get the doors latched. My father's strength saved my family, and my stupidity nearly got my family killed, freezing in the face of the storm.

I knew what this man was feeling, but this was not the time. They needed to move now!

"Tell me where there is a building with a basement?" I hollered at the man. Our lives now hung on his answer.

"If we head out the back door, we can cut across the lot and into the alley. Herschels' Ice Cream has a storage basement. We can get in through the rear door," the man shouted.

"Then let's move before it's too late," I told him, pulling the attendant to his feet.

We rushed out and across the lot, the force of the twister trying desperately to suck us in. I held onto the attendant, he held tight to me, and together we resisted the storm's draw. A chain link fence separated the lot from the alley, but the attendant knew of a breech. The metal posts and fence rattled violently in the torrent as we approached. He slithered through and then pulled the fence back so that I could, too, his hands and arms straining as he did. The wind knocked us off our feet more than once as we struggled to reach the storage basement.

The attendant reached the stairwell first, stumbling and falling about halfway down. As I reached the stairs, I stopped for a second to glimpse back, only to see the garage being ripped to shreds like it was made of paper with chunks tossed out in all directions. The attendant, finding the basement door locked, began banging on it wildly. As I reached him, the door swung open, and we both fell in, landing in a clump on the cold concrete floor.

I heard the door slam shut and felt someone trying to help me to my feet. Just as I did, the building began to shake. Loud bangs and crashes heaped one upon the next. I heard numerous screams surrounding me in the darkness. The thunderous voice of the storm quickly drowned everything out. I held on to whoever had helped me to my feet, praying for my life as most agnostics do in the face of their own mortality. It always amazed me how quickly one can become a true believer.

When the storm finally ended, I realized I was still holding onto the person who had helped me up, and that person seemed much too familiar.

"Becky?" "John?" "Becky?" "John?"

"What the hell are you doin' here?" I asked, shocked to find my old girlfriend in the basement of an ice cream parlor in nowhere Pennsylvania.

"I was coming up to New York to surprise you when I got caught in the storm," she answered. "The road led me here, wherever here is!"

"Why are you here?" she asked, and I'm pretty sure she was thinking the same thing.

"It's a long story, but I'm happy and upset that you're here," I replied.

I kissed her, and all those feelings flared in sparks racing through me as if we were back in Kansas again. I guess I never really knew how much I felt for her and how much I'd missed her. There had been many one-night stands and two-month relationships, but never another Becky. Now, back in my arms, I decided then, and there I would never let her go again.

The attendant, along with some other men, managed to pry the door open to find the stairwell filled with debris. We carefully dug our way out. Once it appeared safe enough, we began helping the others up the stairs. The group clustered in the alley, aghast at the sight of their town in ruins.

Where some buildings seemed untouched, others were flattened. Small fires dotted the downtown and cries for help echoed along Main Street and from the narrow side streets. The group, which numbered about twenty, split up into teams of two and three. We began going door to door to find survivors and help the injured. The mayor, the town's sheriff, and deputy staggered out of a severely damaged courthouse along with a handful of city employees. Those who were not injured joined in the rescue efforts.

I can't be sure how many hours passed before we heard the first sirens of ambulances wailing down through the foothills. Two helicopters swooped down over the town. Shortly after, a National Guard truck accompanied a team from the Red Cross onto Main Street. Becky ran up to the officer who seemed to be in charge. I was busy helping an older couple whose antique shop once stood at the end of the block. Both were shaken and afraid but thankful to be alive, particularly after looking back at what little remained of their store.

Always the pit bull, fiery Becky took charge of the situation, directing the first responders to those in most need of care. Some had to be airlifted to either Uniontown or a hospital in Pittsburgh. A field hospital set up by the Red Cross tended to the majority of the injuries: mostly cuts and abrasions, some broken bones that needed splinting; they even aided a dog who had been hurt, pulling its owner to safety after a fallen tree crushed his car.

Twenty-five people lost their lives that day: some townspeople, some tourists. They were actually very lucky. The death toll could have been much higher. The radio announcements, although they were very late, managed to alert enough of the small population to find appropriate shelter.

A year later, on the anniversary of the storm, the town unveiled a memorial in the public square dedicated to these poor unfortunates. I know because

I was there along with Becky. She, too, received commendation.

Becky had endured the same storms I had. It was she who herded those people into that storage basement, probably saving all their lives. However, we hadn't come back to town for the ceremony. The truth is, we never left. Becky and I decided to make Wyndam our home. Here, I would write my first bestselling novel, **'Twisted Skies'**, a true account of my survival through three tornadoes. A few years later, it made it to the big screen, starring Scarlet Johansen, and, ah, who cares. Scarlet Johansen was in it. How cool is that?

Becky made the city council, where she championed many bills to provide greater preparedness for the township. She worked with state representatives to get funding for storm shelters to be built and the installation of early warning sirens. She took it upon herself to hold training classes for the community, teaching them what to do in a state of emergency, not just storm emergencies.

It took time for it to heal, but eventually, Wyndam returned to its status as the quietest little town in the US of A. Tourists rediscovered its tranquil, almost meditative atmosphere. New shops replaced the old, although the faces rarely changed. Jasper, the gas station attendant, found the remains of my Mercury Montego caught in the cruck of an old oak tree just north of town. It took him nearly a year, but he somehow managed to restore it to its original condition.

We couldn't help but become friends, reminiscing about that day often. He knew I had saved his life, but he never thanked me for doing so, and I never needed a thank you. We would sit in our Adirondack chairs, a cooler full of longnecks between us, staring out across the river into the clearing. With the first bottle, we'd tap the necks together, the ping resonating well into the night. We transcended to the clouds and to the day when fury fell and changed our lives forever.

I guess that's the way it is. The storm tore apart a town, but brought together the people who were stronger for it. Relationships, like many things in this life, need a catalyst. Sometimes, it's just a push, and unfortunately, sometimes, the push has to be a shove. It is more how you deal with the occurrence than the occurrence itself: learning and growing, realizing what's important.

Welcome to Wyndam, population three-hundred and twenty-five, give or take.

The End

"Morpheus"

Morpheus in the mad portrayal

Enters my dreams

Through a door in the darkness.

His grin, ear to ear,

Is as broad as an ocean;

His eyes, pale white,

Shine as bright as the moon

He scratches his beard

As he takes in the moment

Before prancing about

Like a show horse at Devon.

He chains the light widow

To a web in the corner

While strange, twisted figures

Dance on ceiling and walls.

He then strokes at the feathers

Dangling down from his belt loops,

"Trophies", he says,
"One rooster, one dove.

It keeps the fowl
from announcing.

The crest of the morning"

A sudden pause as he ponders,
His eyes, wicked and shifting

From the left to the right.

"Sleep gives me life!" he shouts.

His tone cautious, measured.

Enough not to wake

Those caught in a dream.

Again, he is prancing,

Delightfully whistling and singing
a song in a language unknown.

A tap on the window

Made Morpheus muddle.

His deep sullen, hush

Cascading in echoes

Down dark fluted hallways

Beyond my heavy eyes reach.

He stands at the window.

Hearing the wind

Through the willow;

Despising the dawn
As she rises to light.

One glimpse, he is gone;

Left the dream to a memory.

Hardly a hope

To be thought of again.

Made in the USA
Middletown, DE
30 September 2024